MANIPULATION, MONEY, AND MURDER

Fiction based on actual events

SHERYL JORDAN

ISBN 978-1-961227-46-0 (paperback)
ISBN 978-1-961227-47-7 (hardcover)
ISBN 978-1-961227-48-4 (digital)

Rushmore Press LLC
1 800 460 9188
www.rushmorepress.com

Printed in the United States of America

PROLOGUE

Knock, knock, knock.

Lee Ann set her broom against the wall. "Who is it?"

"It's me, baby," Xavier said.

Lee Ann straightened her old housecoat and opened the door. "Hey, I thought you weren't getting out until tomorrow. I was just cleaning up in here."

Xavier pushed past the open door. His skin was the color of caramel; he had almond-shaped, hazel-brown eyes and nappy brown hair. "I wanted to see for myself what you've been up to while I was locked up."

"Oh, really?" Lee Ann sat down on the sofa. "I haven't been up to anything. Just working and hanging out with my family sometimes."

"Yeah, really, bitch? I heard you been fuckin' that dark-skinned nigga from upstairs," Xavier snarled, his teeth clenched like a mad pit bull.

"I haven't been fucking nobody, baby. I wouldn't do that."

Xavier moved closer and loomed over Lee Ann. "*Yes*, you have. I know everything you've been doing. You're gonna sit there lying to me?"

Before Lee Ann could protest, Xavier's punch landed on her right eye.

Stars exploded all around Lee Ann. Her eye felt like it was on fire. She instinctively covered it with one hand while holding out the other to ward Xavier off. "No, stop!"

"You think I would just let that shit go? Hell no, I won't!"

Bam! She felt blood dripping from her mouth as the second punch knocked some teeth loose. Xavier dropped his weight down on top her.

"Please stop," Lee Ann begged, sobbing uncontrollably. She swung blindly at Xavier. Xavier's fists pounded her in the face and all over her body for what seemed like hours. Lee Ann pulled into a tight ball in a feeble attempt to shield her body.

"I am going to make sure you never fuck another nigga as long as you live," Xavier said. He ripped her panties off and reached for the broom.

PART 1

XAVIER

CHAPTER 1

"Xavier! Wake up, boy!" said Lula Mae Hudson. "Run to the stand for me."

"Aw, ma! I'm tired, it's Saturday morning. Can't I sleep a little longer?"

"No, I need some cigarettes now. Go on. You know what to do."

"Why do I have to steal cigarettes again?" Xavier asked. "Didn't Pops get paid Friday?"

His mom snorted. "That no-good alley cat pissed it away on craps."

"Ma, I can't con 'em anymore. I'm gone get caught and then I'll get in big trouble."

"Boy, you'll do just fine. Now go on and get me as many as you can."

Xavier finally got up and went into the bathroom to brush his teeth and wash up. At age seventeen, Xavier stood about five feet eleven inches tall. His square jaw and fit body meant he always had his pick of any girl at school. And he hated being broke. He hated his lazy parents and their shitty house. He vowed that when he got older, he'd always have lots of money.

Xavier got dressed and left the house. Walking down the street, he ran into his two best friends, Henry Abbott and Joshua Tillman. Henry and Joshua were cousins whose families were very close. Henry, the older cousin by a few months, was a husky five foot ten. He had smooth, dark skin. Joshua had skin like milk chocolate and stood a lean six feet. They both shared the same dark, curly hair.

The three teens chatted for a short time, and then Henry and Josh left. Xavier watched his friends head over to the park. He wanted to go, but he was stuck hustling cigarettes for his mom. He vowed to himself again: when he grew up, he'd always have money. He wouldn't piss it away on rigged craps games like his loser dad or beg for it like his fat-ass mother. He thought, *I have to come up with a plan so I won't ever have to say, "I ain't got no money."*

Xavier approached Mr. Smith's stand. He couldn't stand the pasty-faced Bible thumper. How could anyone let their hair go that gray? The chump should color it or at least wear a hat. Even at seventeen, Xavier stood almost a half-foot taller than the man.

"Hey, Mr. S.," Xavier said. "How you?"

Mr. Smith narrowed his eyes. "Fine, young man. How is your mother?"

This cracker didn't care about his mom, but Xavier would play along. "She sick, ya know."

"I hope it's nothing serious."

Xavier picked up a copy of *National Geographic* and thumbed through it, looking for naked pics. He wanted to grab a *Hustler*, but he figured the old geezer would have a heart attack. "Naw, just the same ol', same ol'."

"Oh, well, that's too bad." Mr. Smith's flat tone put a lie to his concern. That was okay—Xavier knew how to win anyone over.

The boy set the magazine down and flashed his best smile. "Thanks for the love. I'll pass it on." The man's face seemed to soften. It was working. Now he just needed to stall until another customer distracted the old bastard. He decided to lay it on thick. "So Mrs. S. still making those wonderful blueberry pies?"

"Yes, she does." Mr. Smith rubbed his hand over his very round belly.

"She makes the best blueberry pie I ever tasted." Xavier spotted the large cigarette box sitting on the back of a table. Next to it was the open cash box, which was usually kept closed and hidden. As Mr. Smith turned his back to help a customer, Xavier looked around, observing the few other people who were out. When he felt no one was watching him, he crouched down behind the table, reached into the cigarette box, and grabbed two handfuls of cigarettes. Stuffing them into his shirt pockets, he looked around and started to sweat. No one was paying any attention to what he was doing. Xavier began to smile and reached into the cash box, grabbing a handful of coins and stuffing them in his pants pockets. He began to whistle as he walked away from Mr. Smith's stand and headed back home.

Man, Xavier thought, *that was close! But I did it; I'm getting to be pretty good at this. It was so easy! Dumb ol' Mr. Smith will never think I did it. I'd love to see his face when he realizes some smokes and money are gone!* He laughed aloud as he reached his front stoop.

As he was about to open the door, Xavier heard his mother yelling at his brothers and sisters.

"You kids better clean up this house before your daddy gets home or else you're gonna get a beatin'! Y'all hear me?"

"Yes, ma'am," all four replied in unison.

Xavier snorted. Yeah, right. Like his old man was going to be home this week. He'd just got paid.

Xavier heard his stomach growl. Shit, he should have swiped a candy bar when he was nicking cigarettes. He went inside, handed his mom half of the cigarettes, and headed for his bedroom.

Lula Mae yelled, "Is this all you got? And what took you so damn long?"

"I had to wait 'til Mr. Smith wasn't watching. Why don't you get 'em yourself next time?"

Lula Mae ran into to his bedroom. "Boy, who in the hell do you think you're talkin' to?" *Smack!* She slapped her son across his face.

Xavier felt the side of his face burn. He curled his fists into a ball. "If you ever put your hands on me again," he growled, "I will kill you."

His mom took a step back, stunned. Xavier pushed past her and out the door. What an ungrateful bitch. He stormed down the steps and out into the yard. Fuck her fat ass and her goddamn cigarettes.

Whatever happened to the mom who threw him birthday parties with cake? *I can't deal with this fucking family*, he thought. *I've got to get away from them.*

Xavier stopped by Pop's Soda Shop to meet up with Josh and Henry. He stepped out of the dying light outside and into his oasis. The white walls with their pink stripes reminded him of candy. "Blue Suede Shoes" was pouring out from the jukebox. Not that Elvis's version, but Carl Perkins's original. Xavier spotted Josh sitting on one of the black vinyl seats at the end of the bar. He plopped down next to him. Henry was at a booth talking to some girls.

"How's tricks?"

Josh stopped spinning a nickel on the Formica countertop and shrugged. "Just waiting for the jukebox to open up so I can play some real music."

Xavier frowned. "Like what?"

"Big Bopper," Josh said.

"You and your goddamn 'Chantilly Lace.'"

Josh flashed a grin. "Nothing's better."

Candace Parker strolled toward them. Her breasts were like twin missiles straining under her white blouse. Xavier nudged Josh and pointed. "That's better," he whispered. Josh stifled a laugh. Henry walked up to join them.

Candace pulled out her pad and tapped on it with a pen. "What can I get you fellas?" The boys ordered floats. Candace went to a back room before making their sodas. Xavier looked up and saw a big metal box with a handle and some sort of lock on it. It looked similar to the safes he had seen on TV. He wondered whether they actually kept money in it and whether they kept it locked—or if it was even a real safe. He wondered how difficult it would be to get into it.

Henry and Josh began goofing around to the music, nearly shouting at Xavier, "Lay off of my blue suede shoes!" Xavier laughed and looked at the door to the back room. He finally had a plan.

CHAPTER 2

Xavier now had a plan for his future. He would rob places for money. Not houses, or individual people, but businesses—stores in particular—because businesses have more cash on the premises. Besides, individual people could potentially identify him to the police.

First he would need to learn as much as possible about safes, vaults, and security methods. He would have to be very patient and careful. He would not use guns; the risks and dangers were too great. Plus, if he ever got caught he would serve more time for armed robbery than unarmed. He could tell no one of his plans—not even Henry and Josh, his closest friends. They were from a family of cops!

Xavier went to school, but he was so focused on his newfound career plan that he stopped concentrating on his schoolwork. He began hanging out at the local stores, and when he could get a ride to Fort Wayne or Indianapolis, he would go to department stores and watch how things were run. He often took the bus to the city, about an hour away.

His mom began to question where he was all of the time; he'd say he was at the library working on a project for school, or playing basketball with Henry and Josh, or looking for a job. He always had a convincing answer for her. He continued to steal cigarettes for his mom, making sure he had enough so he could sell them to kids at school and in the neighborhood. He saved all the money he could for rides and bus fare to the city.

One day, during lunch at school, Josh asked, "Man, where do you go after school all the time?"

"Man, I'm looking for a job that'll pay me enough to get my own place. There's a lot more jobs in Nap than in small-ass Marion," Xavier replied.

"That's great—I think you'll go far with whatever comes your way, because you are so desperate!" laughed Henry.

"Shut up, stupid," Josh said to his cousin.

"Yeah, just because your fucking mommy and daddy take care of your ass, you wanna make fun and shit!" Xavier yelled, stepping closer to Henry. "I'll show you something funny when I knock all your teeth out your mouth!"

"What's wrong with you? I was only horsing around," Henry said, not backing down from Xavier.

Josh stepped between the two friends. "Whoa, what are you guys doing?"

"This fool thinks everything is so damn funny!"

"Look, I'm sorry, man. I didn't know things were that serious for you," Henry said. He added, "I heard you can get extra money in some jobs, in sales."

"Yeah, they call it commissions," Xavier explained. "It's when they pay you a percentage of the amount you sell. Some jobs pay you low hourly wages plus commissions."

"Wow, how do you know all this?" asked Josh.

"When I go to stores, I talk to the people who work there. Sometimes I even go to job interviews."

He wasn't actually applying for jobs, but he was casing out the stores. He used his problems at home with his parents as a tool to develop patience. He had also been going to the library to research as much as he could find on safes—how they were constructed and how they worked. He read books on famous, historical robbers and outlaws.

"That's kind of weird. I never saw anyone go through so much to try to get an everyday, run-of-the-mill job," said Henry. "But if that's what you feel you gotta do, it's cool."

Just then, Monica Jones walked up. "Hi, guys!"

"Hey, Monica, what's goin' on?" said Josh.

"Not much. I've come over to your house several times in the past week, Xavier, but you ain't never there. What's going on?"

"Oh, I've just been trying to find a job so I can move out on my own."

"That'll be nice, to have your own place in a couple years."

"Yeah, sooner than that if possible. I plan on saving up a lot of money so I'll never be without the stuff I need and want."

"Hey," said Josh, "are you guys going to the dance at the armory Friday night?"

"I am if I don't have to babysit my little sister and brothers," Monica said. "Are you going, Xavier?"

"I don't know. Are you gonna make it worth my while?" Xavier flashed a devilish grin.

"Me being there should be enough to make you want to go— but you'll have to show up and see."

"Baby, a man got needs!" Xavier laughed. "I probably will go." *If I'm back in time from the city, that is*, Xavier thought.

The bell rang, so they all said their good-byes and headed off to their next classes. As Xavier walked to his speech class, he thought about how he really liked Monica. He felt he could marry her one day, if his future went as planned. He and Monica had kissed and fooled around a bit, but they never went all the way. One day they would, he thought—but for now he had to keep moving forward with his plan and test out the strategies he was learning.

When Friday came, Xavier couldn't wait for school to get out. He planned to go into the city to do some more "job" searching. It was a warm sunny day, so he left school two classes early and caught the bus.

In the city, he went in a department store and pretended to browse the clothes. Xavier noticed two salesmen watching him the entire time. He was also watching them, learning their routines. He even boldly asked one of the salesmen what type of material a particular shirt was made of.

Eventually Xavier left the store and headed to another down the street. This one was having a sale, so it was crowded and no one paid much attention to him. He browsed around for a bit and spotted a shirt and pair of pants that would look nice for the dance that night. He carried two identical sets of the clothing into the men's fitting room. He stripped down, put on one set of the clothing, and then put his street clothes on over the new items. He carried the others back out of the fitting room.

A salesman approached, and Xavier's heart began beating faster. "Would this be all for you today?"

"No," Xavier said, "they didn't fit that well on me. I'll keep looking around."

"Where are the other clothes you took in? You had more than this." The salesman eyed Xavier suspiciously.

"I, um, must have left them in the room." Xavier was getting nervous. *That fag was really watching me the whole time!*

Tsk. The man sucked his tongue as he headed toward the fitting rooms. Xavier was halfway to the exit when he heard someone yell, "Stop!"

He turned to see a scrawny store security guard lunge at him. They tussled on the floor. Xavier punched the man, got up, and ran out the door and up the street. He ran until he was blocks away, in a different part of downtown.

Xavier finally stopped running and went into another store where he "shopped" a little while longer, watching the workers and taking in their routines. He asked a saleswoman if they had a public restroom; she directed him to the back of the store. As he reached the bathroom, he saw another closed door holding a sign that said "Private." Xavier turned the knob; it was unlocked. Inside, he saw a large, vault-like safe. He stood staring at it, memorizing the style, make, and model. He was so enthralled with the safe he barely heard a man say, "May I help you? This is for employees only."

A muscular security guard stood to Xavier's left. "Uh, yeah, I was looking for the restroom."

"Go down one more aisle and turn left. It's to the back on the right-hand side."

"Okay, thanks!" Xavier rushed away and entered the bathroom, going into a stall to relieve himself and catch his breath.

After he finished, he left the store and headed to the bus stand to go home. He couldn't help smiling when he thought about that big, shiny safe. He pictured the huge metal box all the way home.

When Xavier got home, he told his mom he was going to the party at the armory. "No, me and your dad are going out, so you have to babysit," his mom said as she applied makeup to her face.

"Aw, Ma! I want to go to the dance; Monica is going to be there and everything!"

"Boy, lower your voice when you talk to me. I don't give a damn who's gonna be there. I finally get to go out with your daddy. I am going and you're babysitting, do you understand me?"

"Yes, ma'am," he mumbled, going to his room to sulk. He had to go; this was his big night with Monica. He knew this would be the night when they finally shared their bodies as one! "Jackie," he called, "come here."

Jackie bounced into the room. Xavier frowned at his twelve-year-old sister. *Ain't no boy going to want her with that messy hair and bony-ass bod.* Oh well, it meant she'd be around on Fridays to cover for him. Xavier flashed a grin. "I need you to do me a favor—but you have to promise not to tell Mom and Dad. I'll give you a dollar!"

"Okay, what do I have to do and where'd you get a dollar?"

Xavier whispered, "You have to babysit while Mom and Dad go out, so I can go to the armory dance. And don't worry about where I got the dollar from."

"Okay, okay!" Jackie whispered back.

"And you better not mess up or else I'm gonna beat your ass, you hear me?"

"Yeah, yeah, just give me the dollar."

When their parents left, Xavier waited until he heard the car drive away. "Jackie," he said, "I'm leaving now, but I'll be back before Mom and Dad."

"Okay, have fun with Monica!" she yelled.

"Smart-ass girl," Xavier mumbled.

He reached Josh's house and they stood on the front lawn, waiting for Henry to arrive. They practiced their coolest and latest dance steps to dazzle the girls with at the dance.

The armory was on the other side of town, so as soon as Henry showed up, they started walking. They began to clown and joke around. It was a warm, starry night. Suddenly, Xavier asked, "You guys wanna have some fun?"

"Sure," Josh said.

Before Henry could respond, Xavier picked up a large rock and hurled it through a second-story window of the house they were passing. He laughed hysterically; Henry and Josh were too stunned to do anything but stare at him. He began running away from the house, with Henry and Josh right behind him. They ran until they were out of breath and could run no more. Josh and Henry looked at each other, then at Xavier. "Are you crazy?" Henry asked, his eyes big and bulging.

"Wasn't that exciting?" Xavier laughed.

"Exciting?" screamed Josh. "What the hell has gotten into you? What did those people ever do to you?"

"He got what he deserved," Xavier said.

"What do you mean by that?" Henry asked in disbelief.

"That ol' man Andrews—the other day he said I walked out of the soda shop without paying for my food, in front of all the people there!"

Suddenly they heard sirens, so they began running again. They hid behind some garbage cans at the side of a house, watching as two police cars drove by with lights flashing and searchlights on. Josh whispered, "Wow, they're looking for us!" After the last car was out of sight, the three boys continued to the armory. A few moments later an ambulance drove past them.

When they arrived, Henry said, "Xavier, look who's at the door."

Monica was there, collecting entrance money. She had on a red dress that fit tightly around her curvy body; her black pumps showed off her sexy legs. Man, Xavier thought, did she look hot in that dress.

"Wow, she looks good!" he said, looking Monica up and down, taking in her beautiful almond-shaped eyes and pouty lips. His gaze paused on her full, round breasts. She turned slightly while talking to a couple; he couldn't help but yearn to feel her tiny waist and big behind. *Ah, man, I have to have that!* He felt a stirring in his groin.

"Hi, guys!" She smiled at Xavier.

He returned the smile. "Hi. You sure look sexy in that dress!"

"Thank you," Monica said as she twirled around and then blushed. "I'm glad you finally made it."

"So are we," mumbled Josh.

"What?" Monica asked.

"Nothing, don't pay him any attention. We're gonna see who all's here. I'll see you later, when you're done taking in the money," said Xavier, eyeing the cash box on the table in front of her.

"Wait," said Monica, "I *know* you see that sign over there. You have to pay to get in here, darling." She flashed a pretty smile.

"Aw, come on baby, just let us in. They ain't gonna miss our fifty cents," Xavier said.

"I can't do that."

"I'll make it worth your while later on," Xavier promised her.

"I'll get in trouble if anyone finds out." Monica tried to sound convincing. She really didn't care if they paid or not. She was just happy Xavier had come.

"Damn, baby, I thought you were cool with us. You really gonna make us pay? Maybe I had you all wrong."

"No, we're cool," Monica said, looking around to see if anyone was watching them. "Damn, just hurry up and go in. You owe me for this."

"Oh, I plan on making it up to you, all right," Xavier said as he licked his lips and looked her up and down once more.

"Just save me a dance!" She smiled.

Xavier smiled back and the three boys walked into the dance. After making a trip around the armory, pausing to speak with friends they knew and girls they wanted to know better, Xavier said to Henry, "Look what I have." He showed his friend a bottle of vodka.

"You're not supposed to have that, especially in here. The bouncers are gonna kick our asses and put us out of here. Where did you get it?"

"Shut up, dummy," Xavier warned. "God, you're such a pussy."

Just then, Josh turned to face them and saw what Xavier was attempting to hide in his pocket. "Where did you get that?"

Xavier ignored his stupid question and went into the bathroom. The others followed. Xavier stood by the window and took a big swig from the bottle. After making sure no one else was in there with them, he took another long swig and passed it on.

"Hey, look," said Henry, "the window's open. We could have snuck in here."

Josh hit him on his head. "You dummy, have you been drinking? It's about ten feet from the ground. Tell me, how would we have gotten in unnoticed? It's not like we could just carry a ladder on our backs and put it up to the win—" His eyes fell on the two muscle-bound bouncers standing behind them.

The tallest bouncer said, "Having fun, boys?"

"Yeah, we are. What the hell do you want?" Xavier had gained a boost of liquid courage.

The other bouncer spoke up. "How did you knuckleheads get in here, through the window?"

"Are you clowning us? We couldn't climb up that high," said Josh.

"We paid to get in," Xavier said. "Ask Monica."

"Whose bottle is that?" The bigger bouncer snatched the bottle from Xavier as he was taking another swig. Josh pointed to Xavier.

"Damn, you're such a liar, Josh," Xavier said. "You know that's your bottle."

"What?" Josh exclaimed. Xavier winked at him. "That's not mine!"

"All right, now, you boys calm the hell down. Did you all pay to get in?"

"Damn, you clowns are so stupid," Xavier said. "We paid to get in just like everyone else. Why are y'all harassing us?"

"Let's go. We'll be checking on whether you paid or not. And you better not be lying, else we gonna take you out back and beat your asses!"

The bouncers escorted the three boys to the front door. Monica was no longer collecting the money. Now an older gray-haired lady was sitting at the table. As they approached, she asked the bouncers, "What's the problem?"

The shorter man jerked a burly thumb at Xavier. "These jokers claim they've paid."

The older woman looked Xavier up and down. She made a disapproving clucking noise. "You boys say you've paid?" It sounded more like an accusation than a question, and Xavier didn't like the way this white old biddy was looking at him. Probably didn't trust him just because he was black.

Xavier gave a curt nod.

"Monica," the older woman said, "come here a moment."

Monica turned around. The color seemed to drain from her face for a moment, and then she composed herself and walked over. "Yes, Miss Lily."

"These boys"—she drew out the word *boys*—"say they've paid."

Xavier looked over at Monica. She chewed her lip. *Damn, she's going to blow it. Just say the words.*

"I ..." Monica began. "I mean ..."

Xavier stepped up. "We gave her fifty cents each."

"Is that right, dear?" Lily asked.

Monica nodded.

"Seemed kind of steep at the time," Xavier said. "We thought maybe she was scamming us. Charging us double and keeping the quarter for herself."

A shocked expression stole over Monica's face. "I would never!"

Lily just shook her head. "It's fifty cents for everyone."

"Yeah, well, you can't trust kids these days," Xavier said. "We done here?"

Lily narrowed her eyes. Xavier was sure that the look meant *I'll be watching you*. Bitch was trying to intimidate him. Good luck with that. Xavier's smile widened.

"Yeah," one of the bouncers said. "We're through."

Xavier turned to walk away, but the bouncer pulled him aside. He showed Xavier the bottle. "We'll be keeping this."

Xavier shrugged. What did he care? He could always steal more.

The three boys left to mingle in the crowd. When they found a spot to stand, Xavier said, "Whew, that was embarrassing!"

"It sure was," Henry agreed.

Xavier turned to Josh. "Why did you rat me out, man?"

"I'm sorry, I guess I got scared and all. They were just there all of a sudden."

"Don't ever do that again," Xavier threatened.

"I won't, I won't. I said I was sorry."

Xavier gave Josh a tap on the head. "It's okay, man, but you better learn to keep your cool."

The three of them danced and partied the rest of the night. Xavier danced mostly with Monica, after she'd finished taking money at the door. While they danced to a slow song, Xavier asked her, "Where did you put the cash box?"

"I gave it to Miss Lily; she locks it up somewhere. Why?"

"I just wanted to make sure it was in a safe place so you won't have your mind on it all night, instead of on me." He brushed his lips softly across her lips and then her cheek. Monica smiled and snuggled closer to Xavier. They danced together the rest of the night.

After the dance, Josh's older brother Tremaine was sitting in his car waiting for them. Tremaine was two years older than the rest of them, but he knew all of Josh's friends. He watched Xavier walk Monica to her friend's car and kiss her goodnight. *I don't know why they keep hanging around that cat. He ain't nothing but trouble.* Tremaine didn't notice the boys approaching the car.

"Hey, Tremaine, can you give Xavier a ride home?" Henry asked, opening the passenger-side door.

"What? You know I don't like that boy," Tremaine replied.

"Aw, come on, Tremaine, don't be so mean," said Josh.

"Okay, but don't ask to stop anywhere on the way."

Tremaine dropped Xavier off first. He felt glad to have that thug out of his car. He worried about Josh and Henry. They were only two years younger, but sometimes they acted like little kids.

Tremaine headed to Henry's house next. On the way, Henry asked Josh, "Have you ever seen Xavier act the way he did tonight? I haven't."

"I haven't either," Josh replied.

"What are you guys talking about?" asked Tremaine.

They relayed the events of the night to him. How Xavier had thrown a big rock through a window of a house, laughed about it, and run off. How he'd snuck liquor into the dance. How he seemed so different lately.

Tremaine thought about it. "Well, Henry, didn't you say he's been having problems at home?"

"Yeah."

"You two should stop hanging around with him. I think he's trouble. I don't want you two involved with him, getting in trouble with him. You need to stay away."

"Yeah, you're probably right," Josh said.

Henry had thoughts of his own regarding Xavier and his trips to the city. The guy was so focused on getting a job that he wasn't hanging around with his old friends much anymore. He never asked them to come along on his trips to the city or the library. Henry had a feeling something serious was going on with Xavier. He'd have to pay closer attention.

CHAPTER 3

On Saturday morning, Henry was up at the crack of dawn. He couldn't stop thinking about the previous night's events. The sun was just beginning to creep across the dusky sky, painting it in hues of orange, red, and pink. Henry went to his bedroom window, watching as the sun began its journey. He was deep in thought about Xavier and what had occurred the night before. He was concerned for his friend and his friend's family. He had to find out what Xavier was doing. He had to talk to him about why he was acting so strange. Still mulling it over, Henry lay back down in bed and tried to get some more sleep. He awoke to his mom telling him to get up; they were hosting a neighborhood cookout with his aunt and uncle.

Henry showered and dressed and went to the kitchen to help his mom and dad. Henry Sr. was in the backyard getting the grill lit with his brother Wilbur and Tremaine. Martha was in the kitchen making potato salad and baked beans while Mary Tillman prepared ribs, chicken, hamburgers, and hot dogs for the grill.

"Good morning, Mom. Hi, Auntie," Henry said as he entered the kitchen.

"Good morning, son."

"Hi, suga'. You seem to get taller every time I see you. How you been doing?"

"I'm doing fine. I went to a dance last night at the armory, so I'm a little tired."

"Did you have fun dancing with all the cute little girls?"

"Yeah, you know it!" Henry laughed. "Mom, what do you need me to do?"

"Go get the ice chests out of the shed and clean them out. Then fill them with ice and the cases of pop your uncle carried out back. Have Tremaine help you."

"Okay," Henry said as he went out the back door. He approached the men standing by the grill. "Good morning, everyone."

"Morning, Henry," said his dad and uncle in unison.

"Hey," Tremaine said, "I thought you were going to sleep all day after the long night you and your boys had!" His cousin playfully punched Henry in the arm.

"Oh, yeah?" asked Henry Sr. "What happened last night?"

"Oh, it was nothing," Henry replied. "Xavier was just acting kind of weird. I guess he has been for the past few weeks; he's having problems at home."

"Y'all didn't get into any trouble, did you?" asked Henry's Uncle Wilbur.

"No sir, he was just not himself, is all."

"Okay. I don't want to hear down at the station that you boys did anything you weren't supposed to." Wilbur was the first black deputy in the town's sheriff's department.

"Oh, you won't." Again Henry thought about what had happened the night before. "Tremaine, help me get the ice chests out of the shed."

"All right." They walked toward the shed and out of earshot of the older men.

"Man, why did you have to bring up last night? You know how our dads are—if they think something's going on, they'll keep questioning us."

"Because I wanted to see you squirm a bit. You are so funny when you don't want to talk about something with them. Don't worry, I didn't tell my dad about the rock through the window or the liquor."

"Thanks, man. I sure am glad no one was hurt. Then I would *have to* tell Uncle Wilbur about it."

"You better be careful when you hang around that kid, or else *you* could get in some trouble," Tremaine advised.

"Yeah, I was thinking about that too. I sure don't want to get in trouble behind his stupidity. I plan on going to college. Do you think we run the risk just by being with him?" Henry tossed some ice into the chest and began filling it with beers and pop.

"You could. But since you guys didn't throw any rocks yourselves, you should be okay." Tremaine picked up one of the ice chests.

"I sure hope so." Henry hoped the cookout would help him forget about last night. It was hard to stop thinking about Xavier and his strange behavior.

Yeah, Tremaine thought, *so do I.*

The two teens finished filling the ice chests and went to see if they were needed in the kitchen. Henry's mom and aunt were busily arranging ribs on a tray. He saw that Josh had finally made it there as well.

"Mom, Auntie, what else can we help with?" asked Tremaine.

"Can you take the trays of ribs and chicken out to the men? We need to get started before too long."

"Yes, ma'am." As Tremaine, Josh, and Henry went to take the meat outside, Stacey and Tracey, Tremaine and Josh's identical twin sisters, came in the front door. They were transporting cakes and pies in an old wagon they still had from when they were little. The girls were talking as they came in the house.

"Can you believe someone would do that?" asked Stacey.

"Girl, it just don't make no sense," Tracey replied.

"What doesn't make sense?" asked Henry.

"Well, someone threw a rock through a window at the Andrewses' house last night," Tracey said.

Henry felt the blood drain from his face. He cast a sideways glance at Tremaine and saw his cousin's judgmental stare. "Was anyone hurt?"

Stacey nodded. "The rock hit Mrs. Andrews in the head."

"Shit," Henry said a bit too loudly.

"Language," his mom called from the kitchen.

Henry ignored her. "Was it bad?"

"Cindy said they took her to the hospital," Tracey said, and then added almost gleefully, "Broke her head wide open. There was blood everywhere."

"You don't know that," Stacey said.

"Bet I do," Tracey countered. "Cindy said so."

"Cindy said no such thing," Stacey replied.

"Stop fighting," Tremaine snapped.

The girls ceased their argument and stared at him.

"Do you *know* if she was hurt or not?" Henry asked, struggling to keep his voice even.

Stacey shook her head while Tracey nodded. A quick stare from Stacey turned Tracey's nod into a shake. Well, at least there was that. But Henry would have to find out. Heck, he might have to say something. He could be in some serious trouble. Still, ratting out a friend …

His mom stepped into the doorway of the kitchen. "You boys going to take those ribs out or just stand there chatting all day? Sun will be down before they get cooked."

"Sorry, mom," Henry said. "Just heading out." He stepped out the door without glancing at Tremaine. He knew what his cousin would say, and he didn't want to hear it.

Henry Sr. had brought out his new record player. Soon enough, other neighbors joined in the fun—there were more than thirty people in the yard, dancing, talking, listening to the music, playing games.

Tremaine and Henry sat at a picnic table, eating their ribs; Stacey, Tracey, and their friend Cindy sat across from them. When Xavier came by, Tremaine muttered to Henry, "Here comes trouble."

"Aw, man, I thought he wouldn't show. He better not do something stupid."

"He won't, not with Senior Deputy Wilbur here!" Tremaine liked to joke about his dad, but he had to admit that he felt safer with his father around.

Xavier came over with his plate of food and sat down next to Henry. The teens all nodded their hellos. Meanwhile, Cindy couldn't wait to gossip some more about Mrs. Andrews. "Guys, did you hear what happened at the Andrewses house last night? Someone threw a rock through their window!"

"Yeah, so what?" said Xavier. Tremaine and Henry stole a quick glance at each other.

"Well," Cindy continued, "the bad part is that the rock hit Mrs. Andrews in the head. She got a big knot on her head and she has a concussion!"

Henry choked on the pop he was drinking. Tremaine glared at Xavier as Xavier asked, "How do you know?"

"Mr. Andrews called my daddy last night while they were at the hospital. Tremaine, I bet your dad knows about it from the sheriff's department."

"He didn't mention anything, but he doesn't usually tell us about his work." Tremaine was still looking at Xavier, who was eating his food extra fast.

"The Andrewses are such nice people; I hope they catch the idiot who did it," Stacey said.

"Nice people my ass," Xavier replied. "Old man Andrews would rather cross the street than talk to a nigga."

"I hate that word," Tracey said.

"Why?" asked Xavier. "It's what he thinks of you."

She shook her head. "He's always nice to me. He gives me penny candy for free."

Tremaine's dad came up behind the three boys, but Xavier didn't seem to notice. "Probably because he thinks you'll steal more if he doesn't," Xavier said.

"Who's stealing what?" Wilbur asked in a booming voice.

Xavier almost jumped out of his seat. Tremaine noticed a hint of fear flash across Xavier's face. That seemed odd. Henry and Josh hadn't said anything about stealing, besides the vodka. *Could Xavier be up to something else?*

"Why are you so upset, Xavier? Are the girls teasing you again?" The deputy sheriff laughed.

"Um, no sir, we were talking about something and I didn't like what they said."

"Yes, Deputy Tillman," said Cindy. "I was telling them about what happened to Mrs. Andrews last night. Do you know about it? It's so sad."

"Yes, I know all about it. We will catch whoever is responsible. You all have fun and don't worry about Mrs. Andrews; she's going to be just fine." Tremaine noticed the worried looks on Josh's and Henry's faces.

Wilbur left the kids and went to talk with Henry Sr. He told his brother about his conversation with the teenagers. "They seemed nervous when I said I knew about the rock incident and that we'd catch the perpetrators. Xavier seemed especially jittery. Tremaine just stared, and Henry and Josh wouldn't even look at me. I'm gonna have to speak with them later on; they definitely know something."

Meanwhile, Xavier finished eating, said good-bye to his friends, and quickly left the cookout.

Later, while the women cleared the outside tables and went to put the food away, Wilbur called to the teenagers. "Hey, guys, come on over here. I need to talk to you about something."

"Yes, sir?" the three answered at the same time. They went over to where Wilbur and Henry Sr. stood.

"So you know about what happened at the Andrewses house, and that Mrs. Andrews was hurt pretty bad, right?"

"Yes, sir."

"I need to know if you saw anything at all last night—anything relevant." The boys exchanged glances and Tremaine nudged Josh to start talking. Reluctantly, Josh told his father about Xavier throwing the rock and what Xavier said afterward.

"Did it ever occur to you that someone may have gotten hurt? Why didn't you come home?" demanded Henry Sr.

"We didn't think anyone got hurt. We didn't see anyone by the window," said Josh, looking at the ground.

"And you're both saying that Xavier threw the rock?" Wilbur asked. "Neither of you did it?"

"That's right, sir," said Henry. "We just saw it happen."

"Dad, what's gonna happen now?" Tremaine asked.

"I'll have to take them all to the station to talk to Sheriff Hale. After that, we will likely arrest Xavier. I hate to do it; he's never been any trouble before. Do you boys know what's going on with him?"

"He's been having problems at home," Henry said. "His dad is gambling and his mom is real mean to him and makes him get cigarettes for her. She's hit him a couple of times that I know of. He says he can't take it there anymore. He's trying to find a job so he can get his own place. I think he was too embarrassed to tell any of you adults."

CHAPTER 4

Xavier looked around the small, windowless interrogation room. It smelled of cigarette smoke. He sat in an old wooden chair at a metal table that had seen better days. The Hudsons had permitted the police to interrogate their son, so while Xavier waited for the sheriff, he tried to think of ways to get out of this mess. *Shit, I am in big trouble. Maybe if I act like I'm real sorry, and play up all the trouble I'm having at home. But damn, old man Andrews is gonna know why I did it. He shouldn't have accused me of not paying for my food last week. Damn it, I've got to think of something fast.*

The door opened and the sheriff, Wilbur, and Henry Sr. walked in. Their presence made the room seem even smaller. The sheriff spoke first. "Xavier, did you throw a rock through the Andrewses' window last night?"

"Yes, but I didn't mean to hurt anyone. It was supposed to just be a joke."

"You think hitting someone in the face with a rock is a joke?" Deputy Tillman tried to control his anger, but his voice was rising.

"No, sir." Xavier looked down at the floor. "It was just supposed to be a joke. It was real stupid of me. I'm very sorry."

"Well, you need to tell the Andrewses how sorry you are. They will be here in a few minutes to press charges against you," Sheriff Hale told him.

Xavier's eyes nearly popped out of his head. "Are you saying I'm going to jail for this?" *Oh shit, I really got to show them how sorry I am.*

"Yes, that's a real strong possibility, boy."

Sheriff Hale and two deputies left Xavier in the interrogation room. The sheriff went to speak with Mr. and Mrs. Hudson, while Deputy Tillman spoke with the Andrewses. Xavier sat in the interrogation room by himself. *Okay, I've got to stay real calm. I can do this. I will act like I'm so sorry. Make myself cry and everything.*

Mr. Hudson stormed into the room with his wife in tow. Xavier could read the fury in his father's eyes. His old man walked right up to him. Papa's body quivered, no doubt with the supreme effort of not just smacking Xavier right there in the station. *Go ahead, do it, old man. Then everyone will see what a shit bag you are.* Papa took a deep breath and then sat down. He stared at his son through bloodshot eyes. "What the hell possessed you to do such a thing?"

Xavier shrugged. "What the fuck do you care?"

Papa drew back his hand, and then he lowered it. He shook his head. "I work so damn hard to take care of you and the family …"

Xavier snorted. Papa ignored him and continued. "And now you go and pull a stunt like this. Do you have any idea how much it'll cost me?" Xavier looked away. "Of course you don't. Well, guess what? It won't cost *me* a damn thing, 'cause you're going to pay it."

"Well, that's good, 'cause it's not like you got any money. I doubt the Andrewses will take your IOUs. Ain't no one dumb enough to take your marker. Not even a cracker." Mama Hudson gasped.

Xavier whirled and fixed his gaze on her. "Maybe I'll just steal some cigarettes and sell them. That ought to pay for it." His mom grew pale.

"What the hell are you talking about, boy?" his father asked.

"Nothing, nothing at all, old man."

Papa Hudson stood up.

Before he could do anything, Sheriff Hale entered the room. He stood while he explained the possible outcomes. "I spoke with Mr. and Mrs. Andrews, and they want to press charges against you, Xavier. The judge could send you to the boys' detention center until you turn eighteen. And they want you, Mr. Hudson, to pay for the broken window to be fixed. I suggested they speak with all of you first, before we proceed with any action." Sheriff Hale signaled for Deputy Tillman to bring in the Andrewses.

When Mrs. Andrews entered the room, Mrs. Hudson gasped and covered her mouth with a trembling hand. She regarded the bandages on Mrs. Andrews's head, the swelling and bruises on her face; Mrs. Hudson began to weep and to say how sorry she was. Mr. Hudson shook his head in disgust that his son did this to the woman standing before them. Xavier looked shocked at the sight of Mrs. Andrews. He hadn't realized the extent of the damage he had done. He was fascinated that one rock could do so much harm—but he tried to suppress his fascination.

Mr. Andrews addressed Xavier first. "Are you the young man who did this to my wife?"

"Yes, I did this."

"You did this because I caught you trying to leave my soda shop without paying for your meal? I don't understand why you would want to hurt my wife like this," Mr. Andrews said in disbelief.

"I was still really mad at you when I threw the rock. I threw it at your window, but I didn't mean for anyone to get hurt at all." *Just get me out of here*, Xavier was thinking. *All this damn talking is giving me a headache.*

"Do you often do things like this?" Mr. Andrews continued.

"No, sir. I wasn't thinking at the time. I am really sorry, Mr. and Mrs. Andrews." Mrs. Andrews gave a weak smile. Mr. Andrews turned his attention to Mr. Hudson.

"Has Xavier ever been in any trouble before this?"

"No, he's usually a good kid. I'm sorry this whole thing happened, and for your wife suffering like that."

"I expect that you will pay for the window to be replaced? It's going to cost two hundred dollars."

"I get paid Friday." He turned to Xavier and wagged a finger. "You're going to have to get a job and pay this back."

"Well, after speaking with you and Xavier, he seems sincere about being sorry, and he hasn't been in trouble before. Perhaps he can work off fixing the window by working at our soda shop—cleaning and helping out around the place. Would that be okay with you and Mrs. Hudson? Of course, I would have to discuss it further with my wife first."

"Yes, Mr. Andrews," said Xavier's father.

Mr. Andrews turned to his wife, who nodded. They were about to leave the room when Mr. Andrews stopped and addressed Sheriff Hale. "I'll call you in about an hour to let you know how we would like to proceed. We are strong believers in giving people second chances. I just hope we won't be disappointed if we do."

"Yes, that will be fine," said the sheriff. "But the judge will still have to determine Xavier's punishment. I'll have to hold Xavier here until he can go before the judge on Monday morning. He'll be charged with vandalism resulting in bodily harm." Xavier wondered if the sheriff was just trying to scare him.

Mr. Andrews called the sheriff back to outline his proposal. The sheriff explained the details to Xavier and his parents. They agreed to it, in hopes that their oldest son wouldn't be put in a detention center.

"Thank you, Sheriff," said Mrs. Hudson. "We appreciate you working with Xavier on this."

"It's not up to me. I hope you both realize the Andrewses don't have to give Xavier this chance—they made that choice. And keep in mind that the judge has to agree to this and can still issue additional punishment."

"Yes, we understand," said Mr. Hudson.

The sheriff turned to Xavier. "Boy, if the judge agrees, I hope you follow through on the deal the Andrewses gave you. I would've had your ass locked up if you did that shit to my wife."

"Boy"? That fat-ass pig! "Yeah, I'm glad it wasn't your wife either, then, sir. I will definitely show up at the soda shop. It'll be so much better than getting locked up." He gave the sheriff a smug smile as he was taken to his jail cell. It was cold, damp, and all concrete except for the metal bars and a very small, dirty window. It was the size of

a closet, and it stunk, but Xavier knew he could survive two nights in the rancid space.

On Monday morning, Xavier appeared before the judge with his parents. The Andrewses and Sheriff Hale were also present. The judge agreed to the arrangement the Andrewses proposed, in which Xavier would work for them to make up for the cost of the window. He added that Xavier would also have to spend two weekends in the Grant County Juvenile Detention Center.

A year passed, and Xavier graduated from high school. After graduating, he began working fulltime in the shop. One day, Xavier overheard Mr. and Mrs. Andrews discussing a building they owned. Although they had paid the mortgage off five years earlier, they were having difficulty keeping the property taxes current on it. They had bought the building twenty years earlier and had leased it to several companies over the years.

"It's just an old warehouse," Mr. Andrews was saying, "but I really don't want to let it go this way. It's just been so hard to find anyone to lease it since we lost our last tenant. I'm going to put it up for sale. If it doesn't sell before the IRS forecloses, then we'll just have to let them have the property."

"I know," his wife replied. "We tried, but realistically, if we lose it, it may be a blessing. The way I see it, we haven't had anyone lease it for over a year now. We're no longer making money on it; we're losing money. It will work out in our favor either way."

"Yes, dear, you're right," replied Mr. Andrews, placing a loving kiss on his wife's cheek.

Xavier, sweeping the hallway, thought about what he had overheard. *Wouldn't it be cool if the place just caught on fire? That would be big excitement in this boring-ass town.* His thoughts went to a TV show he'd seen a few days ago, a western: *Gunsmoke.* One of the bad guys blew up the store of one of his enemies, using gunpowder and dynamite. *I could burn the building down. I could use gasoline. I'd have to be able to get in and out of the building fast. I'll have to check the building out before I actually do it. I love fires—they're so amazing and destructive!*

A few nights later, Xavier went to the old warehouse and checked out the building. Around back there was an old window that was big enough for him to climb through. The building was in an extremely secluded area. No one would see him if he parked his car down the road, away from the building, and walked to it.

The next night, around midnight, Xavier retrieved the jug he had filled with gasoline the night before. He drove past the warehouse, checking to see if anyone was there. He found a secluded place to park his car so that it would go unnoticed if someone passed by. Jug in hand, he headed for the warehouse.

When he arrived, he quickly ran to the back of the building and broke the window with a brick he found on the ground. He placed the jug of gasoline just inside the window on a countertop and knocked down the remaining jagged glass with the brick. Then he raised himself up through the window, tumbling onto the counter, careful not to cut himself on the shards of glass.

It wasn't a very big building, so it would burn down quickly. Xavier rummaged through the place, looking for papers or something else he could douse with the gasoline. He found some crumpled paper and old work rags in the back. He put the rags in a pile and scattered the papers all around. He poured gasoline on the furniture and some welding equipment and a forklift. He set the jug with the remaining gasoline across the room from the rag pile, to give himself time to get back out the window.

Xavier looked around, and then he pulled out his matches. He struck one but was so nervous he accidentally blew it out. "Shit," he said aloud. "Come on, Xavier, calm down. You can do this." He struck the second match and carefully lit the rest of his matches from it. He dropped all the lit matches onto the rags. He stood watching the fire grow from the rags and spread to the papers, burning quickly across the floor.

Xavier ran to the countertop, jumped onto it, and scurried out of the window. He turned to see flames engulfing the interior. "Wow!" he said out loud.

He ran back to his car and drove around for a few minutes. Eventually he heard sirens close by and saw people walking in the direction of the warehouse. He rolled down his window and pulled up beside a group of teenagers. "What's going on?" he asked them.

"That old building down the road is on fire!" one of the teenagers said.

Xavier found a place to park his car out of traffic. He began walking toward the warehouse, joining other curious onlookers. Approaching the building, he saw that the whole thing was in flames. He was in awe, looking at the fire. *This is so cool.* He turned slightly and bumped into a fireman.

"Watch where you're going and stand back," the firefighter told Xavier.

"Oh, excuse me. I've never seen a fire like this," Xavier replied.

"It's one of the worst ones we've had around here in a long time."

Just then, the Andrewses arrived. Xavier took several steps backward, into the crowd, so they wouldn't notice him. "Dear Jesus," said Mr. Andrews, "how did it catch on fire? The insurance company is going to think we had something to do with it!"

"Oh, honey, it will be all right," said his wife. "Remember, the Lord works in mysterious ways."

The fireman who'd spoken to Xavier was rushing toward the other firemen with hoses. He took two steps and *BOOM*! The building exploded.

Mrs. Andrews screamed and clutched her husband. They stood looking on, not sure they believed what they were seeing.

"What the hell happened?" said the fireman. He ran to the firemen closest to the building, checking to make sure no one was injured. One had been hit with some flying debris; he looked like he had minor injuries, cuts and scrapes. No one else appeared to be hurt; it was a miracle.

Nothing was left of the building. What hadn't burned in the initial fire had been incinerated in the explosion. Everyone stood in shock, looking at the pieces of building scattered throughout the parking lot and into the street.

Xavier was still watching all the commotion. He smiled at the thought that he had done this. He could feel his courage growing. It was time, he thought—time to do what he'd planned almost two years ago, to start his life of robbery!

CHAPTER 5

Xavier drove around casing out different businesses—mainly stores. He was trying to decide which one to hit first. He decided on the local grocery store. He had shopped there many times and gotten a glimpse into the back office; it held a safe that was similar to the one at the soda shop.

He discreetly parked in a lot across from the store and just watched for a while. Eventually he went in, pretending to shop while he secretly monitored the security guard and the cash registers. Watching their routines, he observed the cashiers being escorted by the guard to the back room whenever they needed to empty their tills and at the end of each shift.

Xavier went home and watched TV to relax. At eleven thirty, he gathered the black bag containing his tools for getting into the store and the safe. He changed into a black shirt and pants. He collected the black gloves, boots, and ski mask he'd purchased several months ago at a thrift store in Fort Wayne.

He drove around the grocery store several times over a twenty-minute span. After making sure no one was in or around the store, he parked his car five blocks away from the back entrance. It was pitch black outside; the moon was hidden behind clouds and there were no stars lighting the sky. As Xavier walked toward the store, he told himself, *Okay—get in, get the money, and get out.*

In less than five minutes he had reached the building, but he saw headlights coming up the street. *Damn it!* He kept walking past the store. A police car slowly drove past, shining a spotlight on the building. Xavier waited until he could no longer see its taillights and then doubled back. He looked around calmly before making his way to the back door. When he felt it was clear, he jimmied the lock, careful not to leave any markings on the door. Within seconds of his arrival, he was inside.

Xavier stood very still, letting his eyes adjust to the darkness inside and making sure no one was there. He went to the back room and took out a flashlight. Shining his light on the safe, he began turning the lock dial painstakingly slowly, listening for the tumblers to fall. He did that for over an hour. Xavier was very patient in obtaining the numbers for the safe combination. He kept reminding himself to remain calm; once he got in the safe he would have his reward.

He had the first number and was working on the second when he thought he heard something move in the front of the store. He remained perfectly still for ten minutes, barely breathing. He started working on the safe again, but he couldn't hear the tumblers fall. After going at it for a couple of hours, he took a break. *Damn*, he thought, *I can't get that second number. I was able to open the safe at the Andrewses' after many tries.* He was determined to get in this safe. He knew there should be some money in it. He continued working as sweat dripped down his face. Finally he got the second number—but was having no luck with the third. He was about to give up when he heard it: *click!* The last tumbler fell and Xavier slowly opened the safe.

Inside, he saw papers, stacks of paper money, and rolls of coins. He took all of the money, leaving everything else untouched. He put the loot in his bag with the tools and closed the safe.

Xavier's heart beat fast; he'd finally done it! He went to the back door, opening it just enough to peek outside to make sure it was clear. He quickly walked back to his car and had just slid inside when he saw a deputy drive by, heading toward the grocery store. Xavier slouched down in his seat, watching the deputy slow down and shine his spotlight on the building. "Oh shit!" Xavier murmured. He continued watching as the police cruiser passed the grocery store. He let out a long breath. He was home free.

He drove around for a short while before proceeding to his apartment. Back at home, he left the black bag in his bedroom closet and went to the kitchen for a beer. He needed something to calm him down. He was shaking so badly he'd barely even been able to get the key into the lock of his front door.

Once his nerves returned to normal, Xavier opened the bag and put all the money on his bed. He carefully started counting it, smiling when he reached $1,500 and still had over half of it left to count. *Whew!* He continued counting for the next half hour. He had $5,700 and some change!

"I did it, I really did it!" Xavier said out loud. "This is going to be easier than I thought." He hid the money under a loose floorboard covered by a multicolored rug. That night he could barely sleep; all he could think about was the money he now had and what his next heist would be.

For the next couple of days, the local newspaper's front-page story was about how the town's major grocery store had been robbed. Apparently the store had been broken into during the night, sometime after closing. There was no evidence of the break-in except that approximately $5,700 was missing the next morning when the store manager opened the safe. There were no markings on the doors or windows to show how the burglar had entered the store. The safe was intact and no fingerprints had been found on the safe, on the cash registers, or anywhere in the store, besides the prints of the employees. The sheriff's department said they would be investigating the robbery to the fullest. They had implemented extra patrols of all the local businesses. At present time they had no leads and were asking for anyone with information to contact them immediately.

Xavier smiled when he read the news. *I did a damn good job at not leaving any evidence. I am good at this! And it's easy money—lots of money.*

Xavier carried on as if he had a real job in the city. He would leave each morning and drive out of town as if he were going to work. In reality he was looking in the neighboring towns for more places to rob.

During one of his excursions to stake out new territory, Xavier relaxed in his Chrysler, watching patrons come and go from Chuck's Bowlarama. He took a drag on his cigarette and held the smoke. The nicotine felt smooth in his throat. The hot air in the car forced sweat to bead on his forehead, but he ignored it. It was a small price to pay for an easy few grand. He watched a young blonde with long white socks up to her thighs stroll out the door. She dropped her keys and had to bend over to retrieve them. A wide grin spread across Xavier's face. *This job ain't bad*, he thought; *it has its perks.*

A loud banging on the hood of his car caused Xavier to lurch forward. His lit cigarette fell into his lap and he scrambled to retrieve it. "What the hell?" he said.

A tall man with dark skin and a gap-toothed grin leaned into the car. "Hey, cat, what you doing sittin' out here in this heat?"

"None of your damn business," Xavier replied.

"Wait, I know you. Aren't you Xavier?"

"Yeah, who the hell are you?"

"I'm T-Bone, man. Nigga, we used to party in Muncie and Kokomo back in the day."

"Oh yeah, I remember now. You and Junebird were bad news."

T-Bone laughed. "Junebug, not Junebird, fool. Yeah, I guess we were." The man nodded toward the blonde who had finally managed to scoop up her keys and resume her journey to her car. "I think you a private dick to see if that pussycat's been faithful."

Xavier ground his teeth around his cigarette. *What the hell is this asshole's problem?*

"Either that," T-Bone said, "or you casing the joint."

Xavier's jaw slackened so much that the cigarette threatened to tumble out again. He quickly regained his composure. "Just finishing my cigarette."

T-Bone shook his head. "Out in this heat? You either one strange cat or a liar."

"Of course you are." Junebug approached Xavier's car. He was shorter than T-Bone and lighter skinned. "We all liars."

"Man, look," said Xavier, "you're a crazy motherfucker. I said I was just finishing this cigarette before I went to grab a beer. What are *you* up to, besides harassing me for sitting in my car, minding my own business?"

"Nothing. We were watching you stake out this place. You should come in with us and get a better picture of the layout."

"I'll go in and have a beer with you," Xavier laughed, "but I wasn't staking out the place."

"Yeah, okay," said T-Bone.

The three of them walked into the bowling alley and sat at a table at the far end, where they could see the comings and goings of the employees. Junebug teased Xavier about casing the joint. He went to the bar to get them a pitcher of beer. When he returned, he asked Xavier, "Where you from? I haven't seen you down here before."

"Marion. Are you two from here?"

"I just moved here from Gary a few weeks ago," T-Bone said. "Junebug is my cousin. He grew up here in Anderson, but he used to visit my family in the summers when we were kids. We both stay here in Anderson now."

"So why did you think I was staking out this place?" Xavier asked.

"The way you were watching the building, we knew something was up," Junebug explained. "You had to be either looking for someone or casing the place. Since you said you weren't waiting for a girl, we figured you had to be checking out the building."

"I was just finishing up my cigarette before coming in, like I said. What were you two doing? Staking it out yourselves?" Xavier saw Junebug and T-Bone exchange a glance. "So you *are* staking it out! When do you plan on hitting it? Have you guys ever robbed before this?"

"You come clean with us, and I'll tell you what we have in mind."

Xavier looked from T-Bone to Junebug as he mulled it over. He wondered what would happen if he had partners. They would have to split the loot three ways—but then he would have a lookout. And they didn't seem like the type to rat you out if caught by the police.

"Yeah, I was checking out this place. No, I haven't done any robberies yet, just considering it," he lied. "What did you have in mind?"

"I'm gonna tell you, but if you leak any of what I'm about to say to anyone I will kill you." T-Bone pulled up his shirt to reveal a .32 tucked into his waistband. "You get me?"

"Yeah, of course I wouldn't say anything. I keep to myself and I'm not a snitch," Xavier promised.

"Well, me and Junebug have been checking out this bowling alley for a couple weeks. We know the way they operate, how often they go to the bank, and that there is a safe. The safe is in an office behind the front desk. The office is locked at closing time and only the managers have the key. A couple times Junebug took out a girl who works here, trying to get the safe combination, but she said only the owners have it."

"Do either of you know how to crack a safe?" Xavier asked.

"Not yet. I'm the planner and Junebug is the expert at picking locks to get us in. He's so good at it, he leaves no trace on the doors at all. We work well together: we've hit more than thirty businesses between here and Gary, and we've never been caught."

"So why do you need me?"

"We need a lookout, so I can work the safe and T-Bone can get the other loot. Plus, with a third guy we can carry a lot more." Junebug's stare didn't move from Xavier's face. He saw Xavier's expression change just slightly at the mention of getting into the safe.

"I don't know about getting into them safes, it seems tough," Xavier said. "When do you want to hit this place?"

"In a few days," T-Bone said. "They're having a tournament next weekend and there'll be extra cash flowing in. We thought we could hit it on the last night of the tournament, which'll be Saturday. They close at midnight, so at about three or four we can come and do it."

"How much money are we talking about?" Xavier asked. "And you just want me to keep a lookout? I told you I've never done this stuff before; I was only thinking about it."

"Yeah, we heard about the store in Marion that was hit a couple of weeks back. The safe was broken into but the police haven't been able to pin it on anyone."

"We figured you chilled out for a few weeks after that job and then decided to come here and see what joints would be good targets. We were talking about it while we were watching you," added Junebug. "But since you say it wasn't you, just a lookout is what we need."

"How much money are we talking about?" Xavier asked again.

"With the tournament plus the regular business, we're thinking we should get close to fifty grand, if not more," said T-Bone.

Xavier whistled. "So we're talking over sixteen thousand apiece?" With that kind of money, maybe he'd have a chance with Monica. A smile crept across his face. "I could deal with that. But don't they have to pay the winners of the tournament out of that money? If the tournament ends on Saturday night, won't we be too late?"

"No, that's the beauty of it—they're having a tournament dinner on Sunday and that's when all the winners will get their rewards!" Junebug said, smiling. "If we hit it Saturday night after the tournament, all the money is ours. We'll be long gone before the awards dinner."

"Okay, but how do I know I can trust either of you not to set me up? I don't know anything about you guys. You could go to the police afterward and say I did it all myself."

"What good would that do us? We need someone who can get inside the safe. We don't want that kind of heat from the cops. What do we have to do to show you can trust us? Tell us, so we can plan this gig."

"I'll think of something. But I want you both to know this: if you cross me up, I promise you will suffer most painful deaths. Do you get what I'm saying?"

"Oh yeah, we hear you loud and clear," T-Bone said. "And if you cross *us* up, I will shoot you in both your kneecaps just to make you suffer so much you'll *wish* you were dead. Do you get what *I'm* saying?"

"Yeah, yeah. Now let's get this shit planned out so we can get paid!" Xavier said. "We should get out of here—but first I need to try to get a look at the safe. Can you go to the counter and distract the clerk while I try to sneak into the office?"

"Sure. Junebug, go do your thing," T-Bone said. "Christine's working the counter."

"Will do," said Junebug with a big smile. He approached Christine at the front counter. "What's going on, beautiful?"

"Not too much," Christine told him, "just working a lot to get ready for the big tournament this weekend. What's going on with you?"

"Not a whole lot. I'm thinking about buying some bowling shoes. Can you recommend some? I don't have a clue about the differences between them."

"Sure, come with me over to the shoe shop. I can show you what we have and you can see what best fits you." She smiled.

"That sounds good." Junebug looked over at Xavier and then followed Christine around the corner to the shoe shop, leaving no one at the counter.

Xavier casually strolled behind the counter, heading toward the office. No one was inside it when he opened the door. At first he didn't see the safe, so he stepped into the room and looked behind the door. The safe was sitting about four feet away. It looked like the same type as the one at the grocery store, only smaller. He wanted to turn the lock to see how it turned. All of a sudden, he heard T-Bone yelling and making a commotion.

"I have been waiting at this counter for over five minutes trying to rent some shoes and get a lane!" T-Bone was yelling. "No one even gave me the time of day! It's because I'm black, isn't it?" As Xavier came around the counter and headed back to their table, T-Bone winked at him.

"Young man, please calm down," said a heavyset man wearing a name badge. "We are shorthanded, and I assure you no one here was ignoring you. We were all busy. I will be more than happy to help you now."

"Never mind now—I'm just gonna leave now. I will never come bowl here again!" yelled T-Bone as he walked toward the doors to leave. Junebug and Christine came out to see what the ruckus was all about. Junebug saw T-Bone leaving and realized he'd better get out of there as well. He saw Xavier back at the table, smiling as he watched T-Bone in action.

"Look, Christine, I need to get going," Junebug said, "but I'll let you know about the shoes. Maybe we get a burger or go to a movie soon, what ya say?"

"Okay, sure. Call me. You still have my number, don't you?"

"Yeah, I still have it. Take care." Junebug left the bowling alley and walked around the corner to the parking lot, where T-Bone was sitting on the hood of Xavier's car.

"Where's Xavier?" T-Bone asked.

"He was still sitting at the table when I walked out. I'm sure he's on his way out. He's probably waiting so we don't all leave at the same time. He seems to be a pretty smart cat!" Junebug added, "You were smart too, creating a commotion like that. I'm impressed!"

Xavier was laughing as he approached the two men. "Y'all are good! I think I'm gonna like working with you."

"Yeah, we had to do what we could so you wouldn't get caught in there," Junebug said. "So now we need to go somewhere and plan this out. I don't want to hang around here any longer."

"Where can we go?" Xavier asked. "Do you all have a car?"

"We're parked down the street. We'll go get it and drive back by this way. You can follow us to our place, all right?" asked T-Bone.

"Sounds good to me."

Back at T-Bone and Junebug's place, they planned the big job for Saturday—just a few days away.

They pulled the job off without getting caught. Junebug was able to get them into the locked bowling alley within thirty seconds of arriving. T-Bone started to get anxious while Xavier was working on the safe, but Xavier told him to shut up or else he would kill him. Xavier got into the safe after only four tries. It turned out the owners of the bowling alley didn't trust banks with their money and kept most of what they made in the safe. When Xavier opened it, they found over $100,000 inside.

CHAPTER 6

Xavier and Monica began dating in 1968. Monica didn't know that Xavier's income came from robberies. He told her he worked in Indianapolis at a factory. She never went to his so-called place of work and never questioned him about it.

Xavier enjoyed being with Monica more than anyone he had ever met, but he wasn't sure if he loved her. He did sometimes get angry with her and had hit her a few times—but still, he felt she brought out the best in him, made him feel so much more of a man whenever they were together. He felt so special when they made love or just held each other close. She shared everything with him, while he kept his big secret to himself. He wanted to share it with her, but he knew he would lose her forever if she found out he was a big-time robber—and he just wasn't willing to give up that part of his life for anyone. That was why he sometimes felt so frustrated with their relationship and took it out on her.

After they'd dated for a few years, Xavier wanted to ask Monica to marry him—but he was conflicted because of the lie. He figured that if he got married, he would seem like a man with a normal life and a regular job. But he struggled because of his secret. He even went to jewelry stores to find a ring he thought she would like. *She'll love it because it's from me.* But even as he picked out the ring, he looked around and automatically began casing the store.

Xavier paid over half down on the ring and made weekly payments on the balance. He didn't want to draw attention to himself, but he also didn't want the store to check his employment records, since he had none. Each time Xavier made a payment, he found himself looking for a safe and observing the employees. He made a mental note to have T-Bone and Junebug check it out as well.

Xavier was very happy the day he went to pay the remaining balance and take the ring home with him. Now he had to decide when to ask Monica to marry him. He wanted it to go well—but if it didn't, he knew he'd have to move on. He decided to ask her dad first, as that was traditional; he had to do everything just right. He got along well with Mr. Jones and wasn't afraid to talk with him. But first he would talk with his own mom and dad, to see what they thought. They also believed that Xavier had a legitimate job in Indianapolis.

He was sitting on his couch, thinking about everything, when his phone rang and interrupted his thoughts. "Hello?" Xavier said.

"Hey, man, what's up?" Henry greeted him.

"Hey, Henry, how are you, man?"

"I'm doing well. I'm gonna be in town in a couple of weeks and wanted to see if we could get together." Henry lived in Chicago now and worked as a civil engineer at a construction company.

"Yeah, man, I'll be around. I want to talk to you and Josh about something important anyway. That'll be a perfect time. Have you talked to Josh lately?"

"Yes, we had lunch last Saturday. What's going on?" Henry's voice quivered. He couldn't help it—he always worried about Xavier.

"I'd rather tell you when you get here. It's nothing bad— actually, it's real good!" Xavier chuckled. "I heard your voice shake!"

"Okay, okay!" replied Henry, laughing at himself. "Do I need to see if Josh can make it at the same time?"

"Yeah, that would be perfect. One of you let me know when you'll be here. You can stay with me if you want. I now rent a three-bedroom house on Boots Street."

"Wow, you're doing well for yourself. I know you were working for the Andrewses full-time at the soda shop for a long time. I heard you quit the shop and started a job in Nap. Where do you work at?"

"Buehler's Corporation. It's a factory that builds precision gears for helicopters. So you'll be here in two weekends, right?" Xavier tried to change the subject so Henry wouldn't ask too many questions about his nonexistent job.

"Yes, in two weekends. I'll call Josh as soon as we get done talking and let him know to call you to tell you if he'll be able to make it or not." Henry noticed that Xavier was avoiding discussing his job. "When I tell him you have something important to share with us, I'm sure he'll want to be there."

"Okay. So how are the wife and kids?"

"We're all doing just fine. Marie is so busy taking care of the boys and the twins. The kids grow so fast; I can't believe the boys are already four and five and the girls are already seven months. Who would have thought me and Marie would have four kids already! I love them all, but I wasn't expecting them all so soon!"

"That's so great!" replied Xavier. "So call Josh and make sure to tell him to call me tonight or tomorrow. I want both of you to be here—but if it doesn't work out, I'll understand. I'll talk with you soon."

"All right, man," Henry said. "Bye."

Before Henry called Josh, he thought for a moment about Xavier. He remembered when Xavier threw the rock through the Andrewses' window, injuring Mrs. Andrews. Henry had a bad feeling about how secretive Xavier seemed about his job in Indianapolis. He didn't know what it was exactly, but he had a feeling he just couldn't shake. He wouldn't mention it to Josh, but would talk to him about it after the trip to Marion.

"Hello?" answered Josh.

"Hey, man, it's Henry. Were you busy?"

"No, what's going on?"

"I just got off the phone with Xavier. He wants us to come down in two weekends to visit. He said he has something important to tell us and he wants to do it in person, not over the phone."

"Any clue as to what it is?" asked Josh.

"No, just that it isn't anything bad, that it's actually something good! I got a bit nervous and he picked up on it." Henry laughed. "He wants you to call him and let him know if you can make it or not. He said we can stay with him; he rents a three-bedroom house on Boots Street now."

"That's great, but you know neither of us can go home and not stay with our folks. They'd all have a fit!" Josh said. "So where does he work now? I know he can't still work for the Andrewses and afford to rent a house."

"He said he works for Buehler's Company in Indianapolis. He didn't say what he does there or how long he's been working there."

"Oh, that's kind of odd, isn't it? Oh well, Xavier always did keep things to himself."

"Yeah, he does tend to do that," Henry agreed. "So do you think you'll be able to make it in two weeks?"

"Yeah, I can go. Do you want to drive down together?"

'Sure, let's drive together. Don't forget to call Xavier and let him know."

"I won't forget. Take care; I'll talk to you soon."

"All right, man."

Two weeks later, Henry and Josh arrived in Marion, Indiana. They spent Thursday evening with their respective families. On Friday afternoon, Henry picked up Josh and they headed over to Xavier's house.

Xavier was waiting anxiously. They had agreed the night before to meet at three o'clock in the afternoon. They would go to dinner after Xavier shared his important news.

Xavier greeted them at the front door. "Hey, guys, come on in!"

"Hey, man, how ya doing?" asked Josh as he and Xavier dapped hands.

"Hey, Xavier," said Henry. "So what's this big news that you couldn't tell us over the phone?"

"Yeah, what is it?" Josh joined in, smiling. On the way down, he and Henry had puzzled over what it could be, and they came to the conclusion that Xavier was getting more serious with Monica.

"Okay, okay. Come on in and have a seat. Do either of you want a drink?"

"Yeah, I'll have a beer," said Henry.

"Me too," replied Josh. "And hurry up and tell us already!"

"Here you go," said Xavier, handing them each a cold beer. "Okay, so as you know, Monica and I have been dating for a little over three years now." Xavier sat in the chair across from the couch where Josh and Henry were sitting. "I'm going to ask her to marry me. I wanted to see how you both felt about it. I didn't want to talk about it over the phone—I wanted to tell you in person."

"I knew it!" exclaimed Josh.

"Yeah, we thought that's what you were going to tell us," Henry said.

"So you think you're ready for this?" asked Josh. "It's a big step—and once you get married, the babies start coming."

"What's that supposed to mean? Just because I didn't go to college like you guys, doesn't mean I can't take care of a wife and a family!"

"Aw, man, no—that's not what I was saying at all," Josh said.

"What the hell exactly are you saying?" Xavier asked.

"I was just trying to say marriage is serious and takes a lot of work."

"Man, fuck you and your babbling know-it-all shit. Why can't you just be happy for me and Monica?"

"I am, but I take marriage seriously. I just asked a question. I see you're still defensive and always think someone's trying to get to you."

"Okay, you guys," Henry broke in. "This is supposed to be a good time—let's not ruin it by arguing. Xavier, I've been married for several years now and it is hard—not only financially, but emotionally. And once the kids come, it's just damn tiring at times."

"So do you think she'll say yes?" asked Josh, trying to smooth things over.

"Yeah, I think so, but I don't know for sure. We've talked about it some before—not serious, though, just 'what if we were married' kinds of games," explained Xavier. *If she says no, I'll just move on to the next broad.*

"Then I think it's great, man!"

"Yeah, did you get a ring yet?" Henry asked.

"Yep, it's right here," said Xavier, pulling a small red-velvet box from his pocket. He opened the box to reveal a beautiful silver ring; in the center was a diamond about one third of a carat in size, with three smaller diamonds on either side. It wasn't a fancy ring; it was actually quite simple. Xavier could have gotten Monica a ring worth a lot more, but he didn't want anyone asking questions about how he could afford it and about his job. He just wanted something nice that Monica would like.

"That's a nice ring," said Josh.

"Yeah, Monica's going to like that!" said Henry.

"I sure hope so. I had it on layaway for almost six months. I'm gonna take her out to a nice restaurant in Indianapolis and ask her there."

"When and how are you going to ask her?" Josh asked.

"I want to do it tonight, while you guys are here. Then we can all celebrate tomorrow if she says yes, and I'll want you guys around if she says no."

"Sounds like a good plan," Josh said. "I'll call you in the morning to see how it went and find out what we'll be doing. I have a strong feeling we will be celebrating!"

"Do you think she suspects you're going to ask her?" Henry asked.

"No, I didn't tell her anything that would make her suspicious. We do stuff together just about every Friday, so that wouldn't make her think anything different."

"That sounds like a good plan," Henry said. "I sure hope all goes well for you tonight."

The three friends finished their beers, reminiscing about the past and talking about their hopes for the future. Xavier was cautious in what he said about his work life.

After Josh and Henry left, Xavier took a shower and dressed for the evening. He arrived at Monica's house promptly at six o'clock. Monica answered the door, looking beautiful in a blue-and-yellow dress.

"Hello, baby, come on in. I'm gonna grab a sweater," she said, smiling.

As they drove the hour to Indianapolis, they sang along with the radio. They talked about how each of their days had gone. Soon they were being seated at the restaurant.

After the waiter brought their drinks, Xavier removed the box from his pocket and got down on one knee, opening the box to reveal the sparkling ring. Monica looked surprised and asked him what he was doing. He smiled and said, "Monica, you know I have loved and cared about you for a long time. Will you marry me?"

Monica was speechless. Tears began to fall from her eyes. "Yes. Yes, I will marry you!" she choked, as Xavier placed the ring on her finger. The workers and patrons in the restaurant all began clapping and cheering. Xavier kissed and hugged Monica through her tears.

They drank champagne and ordered their dinner while planning for their big day. But when the waiter brought their food, it wasn't what they had ordered.

"What is all this? It's not what we ordered, you incompetent idiot!" Xavier yelled at the waiter.

"I'm sorry," said the waiter, picking up the plates, "it's for another table. I just don't know where my head is at tonight."

"Seems to me it's up your ass. You need to hurry up and make this right." Xavier sneered at the waiter.

"Honey, it was a simple mistake," Monica said, blushing with embarrassment. "Why are you being so rude about it?"

"He's ruining our special night, and I don't like it."

"Please calm down. You're overreacting and making me nervous."

"Okay, I'm sorry. I just wanted tonight to be perfect. Will you still marry me?" Xavier chuckled.

"I will." Monica smiled. But she was thinking, *He needs to keep that temper under control. I saw something in him tonight I haven't really seen before.*

CHAPTER 7

Monica and Xavier set their wedding for the first of August. They planned to hold it at Monica's parents' home in the backyard. They invited all of their close friends and relatives.

Three weeks before the wedding, Xavier hooked up with T-Bone and Junebug to plan their next robberies. Xavier wanted to hit at least two more businesses before the wedding day. They met at T-Bone's place in Anderson. Junebug answered the door. "Hey, man, come on in," he greeted Xavier.

"Hey, man, what's going on?" Xavier asked.

"We're just thinking it would be best to hit the jewelry store first, then hit the warehouse in Indianapolis. Do you want a drink?" added T-Bone.

"Sure, what do you have?"

"I got some beer, scotch, and whiskey."

"I'll take scotch on the rocks and a beer."

"What do you think of our plan?" asked T-Bone as he handed Xavier the drinks.

"It sounds good, but I think we should step it up a bit. I think we need to hit something big, like a bank."

"Man, are you crazy?" Junebug said. "We don't do hits on a bank! That's some serious time if you get caught on a bank hit. Why do you want to hit a bank all of a sudden?"

"You both know I'm getting married in a few weeks. I won't be able to do as many hits once I get married—so I want to do a big hit and have plenty of money to tide me over for a long time."

"Well, I guess that makes sense," said T-Bone. "But we haven't planned on a bank job yet. I don't know if we're ready for that. I mean, the banks have more security, and they're harder to try to get into. If we case a bank, it will definitely draw a lot of suspicion on us."

"Maybe not, if we are extra careful. I *have* to step it up, though. I've already been looking at a couple of the bigger banks—one in Nap and one in Fort Wayne. We can get in and out the same as we do at the joints we've been hitting. The safes are basically the same, just bigger. And I know our man Junebug here can get us into any door in the world, except maybe Fort Knox."

"I say we do it," Junebug said. "We only live once! We'll never know how far we can go if we don't try it."

"Okay, so it's agreed," Xavier said. "We will hit the First National in Nap. We need to go and scope the place out over the next few days. We should go separately so we're not seen together. I was planning on going tomorrow morning. Me and Monica have some things to take care of for the wedding, and I'll suggest we go to the bank and look into opening a checking account."

"Okay," agreed T-Bone and Junebug in unison.

Junebug offered, "I'll go the day after tomorrow to get a look at the locks on the outside doors and see what I'll be dealing with on the inside."

"All right," added T-Bone, "then I will go tomorrow evening to see what types of patrol the police or security are doing, and I'll eyeball their procedures for closing up the place. I'll go back later at night to see if there's any night patrol. I'll have to do that for a few days to figure out their routine. I can start on that tonight, actually."

"So let's all do our stakeouts and meet up in about four days. That should give us all time to find out all we need to know about the bank. We also need to think about where to hit after that. Depending on how this hit goes, I think we should hit the bank in Fort Wayne," Xavier said. T-Bone and Junebug agreed.

Over the next four days, the three men cased the First National Bank as planned. Xavier took Monica there the next day under the guise of possibly opening an account together after the wedding. They had gone to Indianapolis that morning to pick out simple floral arrangements for the wedding and reception. Monica had chosen a rose bridal bouquet, with roses of yellow, peach, pink, and white mixed with white lisianthus and stephanotis flowers. For her bridesmaids' bouquets, she'd chosen arrangements of yellow, peach, and pink roses with touches of baby's breath. On the way to the bank, Monica asked Xavier if he and the guys had gotten their suits yet.

"Honey, did you hear me?"

"Uh, no, what did you say?" asked Xavier.

"I asked you if all the guys got their suits and shirts. You were a million miles away. What's on your mind?"

"Aw baby, I was just thinking about our big day," Xavier lied. "We all have our suits and shirts ordered. I'll pick up Josh's and Henry's when the store tells me they're ready." Xavier was really thinking about the bank; he was hoping it would be an easy in-and-out job. He was thinking about what he needed to look for while they were there.

"I know," said Monica, smiling, "I can't stop thinking about our wedding either, I'm so excited. I hope everything goes right. I can't wait to taste the cake Mrs. Andrews is making us. I didn't even know she baked wedding cakes; what a nice surprise!"

"Mmm, yes, she bakes the cakes and pies for the soda shop all the time, and they are so good. I'm sure our wedding cake will be real tasty and pretty," said Xavier as he pulled into the bank parking lot.

He held the door open for Monica as they entered the big brick building of First National Bank. Xavier noticed the high ceilings and shiny floors. The walls were beige, the desks and counters dark brown. The floors were natural hardwood in beige and tan tones. He looked around causally, trying to determine where the safe or safes were located. He assumed they were behind the two huge doors to the right of the teller windows. He watched the doors, hoping someone would go in or out so he could see what was behind them. No one did.

Xavier, T-Bone, and Junebug staked out the bank as they had discussed; everything went according to plan. They met up a few days later to go over the details of the robbery. They decided to do it on the upcoming Friday night.

On Friday, they drove separately and planned to be inside the bank by two o'clock in the morning. Each man was dressed all in black with gloves and ski masks in their pockets. They approached the bank from different directions so if they were seen, no one would know the three of them were together. As they reached the bank, they put on their ski masks.

Junebug went to work on the lock of the back door and got them inside in record time. It took him only thirty-seven seconds to open the big steel door. They entered the dark, open, spacious bank. An alarm began sounding. T-Bone had noticed the control panel when he'd cased the bank earlier; he rushed to the panel and disarmed it by cutting the wires. He quickly turned his flashlight off. They all left their flashlights off, waiting a few minutes for their eyes to adjust to the dark. They quietly looked around the space, making sure no one else was present. When they were confident it was only the three of them, Xavier and T-Bone headed for the back rooms.

They looked in each of the back rooms until they came upon the safes. There were three safes in all. Xavier began working on the first one. He spun the lock slowly, listening for the tumblers to fall. The first go around, he didn't hear them. The second time, he strained to hear and finally picked up on the clicking of the tumblers. He got the first number and was trying to get the second one when they suddenly saw a beam of light shine through a front window.

They lay as flat to the floor as possible and remained perfectly still until after the light passed. They didn't move for more than five minutes. Once they thought it was all clear, Xavier went back to opening the safe while T-Bone and Junebug cautiously explored the front of the bank to see what was going on. They didn't hear anyone inside, but they could see a cop outside, doing his rounds.

"Man," whispered Junebug, "I thought you cased this place out all night. You said we were clear after one o'clock."

"I know, that cop must be late making his rounds. I sat out there and watched four nights in a row. The last check was always at one."

"You go back and see how Xavier's doing. I'll keep watch up here."

"I still can't believe that damn cop is out there. Shit!" T-Bone whispered. He returned to the back rooms and found that the first safe was open and Xavier had started working on the second one.

"How's it going?" asked T-Bone.

Xavier gestured at the open safe. "One down. Why don't you start loading that loot into your bag." Xavier didn't like T-Bone hovering over him while he worked. He watched T-Bone check out the large stacks of cash with wide eyes. T-Bone began loading the contents of the first safe into his duffel bag. When he finished emptying the safe, he went back over to where Xavier was still working on the second one. Xavier could feel T-Bone's eyes on his back as he worked. He was getting frustrated; his forehead began to sweat.

"Hey Xavier," T-Bone said, "why don't you take a little break? You need to calm yourself so you can focus."

"I almost had it. One more time." Xavier went back to focusing on the lock. He thought he had it, but when he tried to open it, the lever wouldn't move. "Damn it!" he yelled. He stood up and walked away from the safe. He wanted to throw something. He paced around for a few minutes, collecting himself.

Junebug came in to see what the yelling was about. He saw Xavier pacing, looking agitated. He tried talking to Xavier to get him back on task. "Come on, man, this safe is no different than the other ones you've busted open. I know you can do it. Look, you got into the first one. Take your time and stay focused."

"Man, back the fuck up and stop talking to me now or I will throw you through that got damn wall!" Xavier yelled as he walked back to the safe and tried again. The other two men held their breath as Xavier returned to work. Finally he exhaled loudly as the safe's lever released and the door swung open.

Junebug immediately began filling his bag with the money. This one had more documents—bonds, certificates and other papers—than cash. He took only the cash and left the documents in place.

Xavier immediately went to work on the third safe. He got it open on the second attempt. They immediately saw that this safe held all cash—it was filled almost to capacity with money! They quickly stuffed the cash in their bags along with all of their tools. They did a quick check of the back rooms and the front area to make sure they weren't leaving anything behind. Once they were satisfied everything was the same as when they arrived—except that the money was now theirs—they carefully began to exit through the back door.

With their masks still on, the three men went out one at a time. Xavier went first; he opened the door slightly, looking around quickly. He then began casually walking to his car, removing the mask when he was sure no one was around. He walked quickly with the heavy duffel bag over his left shoulder.

T-Bone came out next, being careful not to let the door bang shut. He too looked around, but waited for Junebug, who had to lock the door. They were just leaving the parking lot when they heard a shout in the distance. They began to run, each man in a different direction toward his car.

The sound of gunshots echoed off the alley walls. "Freeze! Police! Stop or I will shoot you!"

Shit, they gonna shoot my ass. Xavier wasn't going to jail. If that meant a bullet in the back, so be it. Xavier dashed down the alley, dodging a lick of garbage that had spilled out of a tipped can. The duffel bag stuffed with cash made it difficult to keep his footing, but there was no way in hell he was tossing aside his hard-earned money. Xavier rushed headlong toward a wooden fence at the far end. It would be a tough leap, but he figured he could make it—and he did.

Xavier had just got in his car when he saw a cop down the street with his gun drawn. *Oh fuck, that looks like Tremaine.*

"Shit, I've been hit!!" It was T-Bone. "Help me up, man, they got me in the leg," he yelled. Junebug ran over to T-Bone to help him run. He grabbed the duffel bag from T-Bone, slung it over his shoulder with his own bag, and half-carried T-Bone as they tried to run faster. They made it to the next block just as they saw Xavier's car coming down the street. He stopped next to them so they could quickly climb in the backseat; he told them to get down. Xavier saw Tremaine come around the corner, spotting his car. He rolled down his window.

"Tremaine, man, what's going on?"

"Did you see two black guys running down the street? One may be shot," Tremaine said.

"Yeah, man, I saw them about a block back, cutting through the alleyway. I hope you catch the bastards."

"Yeah, thanks, man." Tremaine took off running in the direction Xavier had pointed.

When they were several blocks away, Junebug sat up and helped T-Bone stretch out his leg. "What the fuck was that about?" he yelled. "You're friends with a cop? Didn't we tell your ass what would happen if you ratted us out?"

"Hey, man, calm your ass down and let me explain. He's the brother of one of my friends. I forgot he's a cop in Indianapolis now. I had to do that, otherwise he would've thought I did the job. He knows my car. I had to throw him off. Trust me, he would have gotten real suspicious if I didn't stop."

"Okay, can you two stop arguing?" T-Bone groaned. "My leg is burning real bad." He gasped and then said through gritted teeth, "Junebug, see if you got something to tie around it to stop the bleeding."

"Oh, yeah, let me look at it. It looks pretty bad; I think the bullet is still in there. You need to go to a hospital."

"No hospitals. Get me home and then you two are gonna have to get it out of me."

They drove to Anderson in silence. They were all thinking about how close they'd come to getting caught and how one of them could have been seriously injured or killed. Xavier was thinking about the lie he would've had to come up with to explain it if he'd been the one who got shot.

They arrived at T-Bone's apartment about twenty minutes later. They got him and all the bags inside, where T-Bone removed his pants and showed them his wound.

"How bad is it?" he asked.

"Well, lie on your stomach so I can get a better look at it," said Junebug. "Um, it doesn't look real bad; I can actually see the bullet, so it's not deep."

Xavier leaned in to get a better look. The bullet had penetrated T-Bone's thigh, but it was near the surface of his muscle tissue. "Aw, we can get that out with some tweezers. You got some rubbing alcohol and bandages? Oh yeah, and you will probably want some whiskey."

"Okay, the bandages and alcohol are in the bathroom," T-Bone said. "The tweezers are in my bedroom on the dresser."

Xavier went to get the stuff out of the bathroom and grabbed a towel, while Junebug retrieved the tweezers and the whiskey. "Okay," Xavier said, "we're all set. T-Bone, drink a lot of whiskey, and maybe we should do this in the kitchen so you don't bleed on the couch. You can lie on the table so we can work faster and have better access to the bullet. Junebug, make sure you sterilize the tweezers on the stove and pour some alcohol on them."

"Ah, let's hurry up," said T-Bone as he took another swig of whiskey, his speech beginning to slur. Xavier took the tweezers from Junebug and poured some whiskey into the wound. *"Aw shit, that burns!* What the hell did you do?"

"I poured whiskey in your wound so it won't get infected. Here," said Xavier, handing the bottle to T-Bone. After he took another swig, Junebug talked to him to distract him while Xavier began trying to take out the bullet.

"So how much money do you think we got?" Junebug asked.

"Oh, I's woo' guess 'bout a million doll hairs!" T-Bone slurred. "I git mo' than y'all cuz I got the bull … bulle … shot."

Junebug chuckled. "We'll talk about that when you sober up."

"Damn, I almost had it! Did you feel anything?" asked Xavier.

"Ah litsle 'tingy, is it out?"

"Not yet. Let me try again."

Xavier once again stuck the tweezers into the open hole in T-Bone's thigh; blood oozed out of the wound and ran down his leg. Finally he got a good hold of the bullet and snatched it out before it could slip from of the tweezers again. Xavier quickly poured more whiskey into the open wound, followed by rubbing alcohol. This time T-Bone barely noticed the pain.

Junebug put a bandage on the wound. He hoped it would begin healing soon so there wouldn't be so much blood loss. He knew he'd have to clean the wound out and change the bandage often until then.

T-Bone slept the rest of the night and most of the next day. While he slept, Xavier and Junebug counted all of the money in the three duffel bags. It took them the rest of the night to count it all: they had $878,755 which was over $290,000 each! That amount would last Xavier for several years—but he was getting such a great high from getting away with these robberies that he knew he wouldn't stop.

CHAPTER 8

The next day, Xavier drove Junebug to Indianapolis twice in order to pick up T-Bone's and Junebug's cars. When they first arrived, they drove around the block a few times to see if anyone was watching the cars. When they were sure no one was paying attention to them or the cars, Xavier pulled up next to T-Bone's car; Junebug quickly jumped into it and drove back to Anderson.

Back at T-Bone's apartment, Xavier parked his car and got into the passenger's side of T-Bone's car, and Junebug drove them back to Indianapolis to retrieve the other vehicle. Again they drove around the block a couple of times, checking to see if anyone was watching. They pulled up and Junebug got out of one car and into the other, and Xavier slid into the driver's seat of T-Bone's car. Just then, Patrolman Tremaine Tillman approached to tell the driver to move along. "Hey buddy, you got move the car, you're blocking traf—Xavier? Why the hell do I keep seeing you down here now, of all times?"

"Hey, Tremaine! I was just helping a friend pick up his cousin's car. We were partying last night and he had way too much to drink. He's still sleeping it off. We didn't want to leave his car here any longer than necessary." *I hope he doesn't recognize Junebug,* he thought.

"We'll talk later—for now you need to move," instructed Tremaine.

"All right, see ya later," said Xavier as he drove off.

Junebug, watching, thought, *What the hell is going on now? Shit, that's the same cop from last night! That nigga is way too close with him. He better not be setting us up—I swear I'll kill his ass. We'll deal with that when we get back to Anderson.* Junebug turned up the radio for the drive back.

Again they arrived back at T-Bone's apartment; both men parked their cars and got out. "Man, what did that fucking cop want again?" demanded Junebug. "You're a little too chummy with him for my comfort."

"Look, man," Xavier said through gritted teeth, "I told your ass, he is my friend's brother. Don't ask me again. I didn't know he worked the area when we picked that bank. I am not trying to go to prison or send anyone else there, either."

"You better not, otherwise you will die. I am not going down because your ass is friends with a cop," replied Junebug.

"Man, stop worrying about it, damn it! I told him we were out partying last night and T-Bone was too drunk to drive home. I covered it," said Xavier. "Now let's go in and check on T-Bone."

"Yeah, okay."

Inside, T-Bone was sitting on the couch watching his small black-and-white TV. "Hey, did you get the cars?" he asked.

"Yeah, we got them," Junebug said, "but that nosy cop showed up again."

"What happened?" T-Bone asked. Xavier relayed the story. "So what is he going to talk to you about later?"

Xavier glared at Junebug. "I don't know, probably about the robbery. To tell me to stay out of the area until the robbers are caught. You guys need to stay calm and let me handle the cop."

"Okay, but nothing wrong better go down," T-Bone said, "or else you'll have a hell of a lot more to worry about besides the cop!" Then he asked, "How much loot did we get?"

"Nearly nine hundred thousand bucks," Junebug said. "That's damn near three hundred each."

"Wow, that was a real big hit! Let's just hope nothing else goes wrong. We had a hell of a night and day. We need to lay low for a while." T-Bone winced with pain. "The bleeding has slowed a lot, but it hurts like the devil. So get this wound all cleaned up and let's get down to splitting up the dough!"

Xavier looked over at T-Bone's leg as Junebug cut off the blood-soaked bandages. The bullet had left a gaping hole the size of a nickel and about two inches deep. The flesh inside was visible, but the bleeding had slowed to a trickle. Junebug poured peroxide into the hole. T-Bone jerked his leg away and howled. "Man, that shit burns! Do you know what you're doing?" He shook his head. "I sure hope this heals fast. I don't know how much more of that peroxide I can take."

"I know," Junebug said, "but you don't want to get an infection and have to go to the hospital. We have to keep doing this until the wound closes up." He continued cleaning out the wound and then covered it with fresh bandages. "Remember what happened to that dude Johnny who was shot in the arm? He tried to take care of it himself and it got infected so bad—by the time he decided to go to the doctor they had to chop his arm right off! I *know* you don't want that to happen with your leg, cuz."

"Yeah, you're sure right about that!" exclaimed T-Bone.

They split up the money three ways, and Xavier left to go home. While he drove back to Marion, he thought about everything that had happened over the past two days. He was worried about Tremaine. Josh's brother had always been a smart guy—probably too smart to chalk up Xavier's appearances near the bank to coincidence. He needed to find out what Tremaine was thinking, and whether he had any suspicions.

Xavier was also thinking about Monica. He'd noticed her acting weird, eating more than usual and feeling sick a lot lately. He thought she was pregnant. *Damn it, she better not be.* He planned on seeing her tonight. He would call and ask her over to have dinner and watch TV.

"Hello?" Monica answered her phone on the fourth ring.

"Hey, baby, how are you?"

"I'm okay, but where have you been for the past two days?"

"I told you, I had to work all weekend—and then I hung out with a couple guys from work. What's with all the questions?"

"Well, you could have at least called me. I … um, I guess I just miss you. It seems like I haven't seen much of you lately."

"How about I come and get you and we can eat dinner and watch television?" Xavier asked. "I miss you too, baby. I just want to hold you all night."

"Okay. What time will you come by?"

"How about five thirty? Decide what you want to eat so we can grab it on the way back to my place."

"That's perfect," Monica said. "I'll be waiting."

Xavier grabbed a cold beer out of the refrigerator and took a long, hard swallow. It was refreshing and what he really needed. He let his thoughts drift back to the previous two days. He was worried about Tremaine possibly connecting him to the robbery. He didn't really care about what happened to T-Bone and Junebug—except if they were caught, he wondered if he could trust them not to turn on him. He knew he would never turn them in; if they chose to snitch on him, he'd need to have a plan to do away with them.

He finished his beer and removed his clothes while he ran a bath. Naked, he walked back to the kitchen while the tub was filling and grabbed another beer. He slowly lowered his body into the hot water and felt his tense muscles begin to relax. He sipped on the beer and closed his eyes. His mind drifted to how he could get rid of both Junebug and T-Bone if necessary. He figured he could get a gun and shoot them both in the head if he had to. *No,* he thought, *that's too risky.* T-Bone and Junebug were always together—and even if he caught one alone, the other would know Xavier was behind it. After all, he'd be the only one to gain anything by them dying. No, shooting them definitely wouldn't work. He took a couple more swallows of beer and began drifting off to sleep while the hot water worked the fatigue out of his body. Suddenly, he sat straight up in the tub. It hit him like a lighting strike. He could set T-Bone's apartment on fire while they slept. That is how he would get rid of them when the time came!

Suddenly energized, Xavier finished his bath and quickly dressed. He hid the money under the floorboard as always, checked to make sure none of his tools or dark clothing were lying in the open, and left to pick up Monica. He was quite pleased with himself; he felt as if he were on top of the world.

Monica was ready and waiting when he pulled up to her home. "Hey, gorgeous, how are you doing?" asked Xavier when she opened the door.

"'I'm good now you're here," Monica replied. She gave him a deep, passionate kiss on his lips.

"Are you ready to go?"

"Yep, let me grab my bag and I'm all yours for the night. I decided I want something from the soda shop for dinner. I want a giant cheeseburger, fries, and a large cherry soda with vanilla ice cream!"

"Whoa, are you going to eat all of that? I've never seen you eat that much in all the years I've known ya!" laughed Xavier.

"Yeah, well, things change and I am really hungry." Monica half-laughed and then her bottom lip began to quiver. Xavier looked at her asked, "What the hell is wrong with you? Why are you crying all of sudden?"

"I don't know. I do this all the time lately. I just start crying for no reason, and the next minute I'm all happy. I think I'm just excited about the wedding."

"Or maybe you're pregnant."

"Oh, don't be silly. It's just my nerves."

Xavier narrowed his eyes. "Okay, if you say so. You better not be. I don't want no damn kids."

"That's not very nice for you to say! But I don't want children yet, either. Anyway, I really don't think that's what's happening. Now, can we go, because I'm really hungry!" Monica handed her overnight bag to Xavier and grabbed his other hand, leading him to his car.

They drove to the soda shop, laughing and making small talk. Xavier's laughter felt forced, but he couldn't do anything about it. He kept thinking about Monica possibly being pregnant. That would ruin everything. When they arrived at the shop, Mr. and Mrs. Andrews and Candace were all working.

"Well, hello, stranger!" Mrs. Andrews greeted Xavier with open arms.

"Hi, how are you?" Xavier asked as he hugged Mrs. Andrews. Mr. Andrews approached the three of them.

"Well, hello, Monica. Hello, Xavier." He put his arm around his wife's shoulders. "What finally brings you around, Xavier?" Mr. Andrews teased.

"We were on our way to my place and thought we'd pick some food up here first. It's been a long time since I've eaten here, and Monica insisted on it!" Candace came up to chat and take their orders and then returned to the kitchen.

"By the way, are you coming to the annual ice-cream social this Saturday?" asked Mrs. Andrews. "It starts at two and goes until six."

"Yeah, I'm coming," replied Monica, "but I don't know if Xavier has to work or not."

Yeah, I gotta work on robbing a joint, Xavier thought. But he said, "I have to work until three, but I'll be there afterward. You know I always like your ice-cream socials."

"Good; we love putting them on year after year. It's a great way to have fellowship with the community and bring people closer together. Personally, I love seeing all the children enjoying all the ice cream they can eat," said Mrs. Andrews with a smile.

Their food arrived and they said their good-byes. When they got to Xavier's house and let themselves in, they went straight to the living room. Xavier turned on the television and they sat on the couch, sharing soft kisses between bites of food and sips of ice-cream soda.

When they'd finished eating, Xavier began kissing Monica's soft lips more deeply but still gently. They lay on the couch with their bodies pressing hard against each other. Monica began rubbing Xavier's backside as his kisses grew harder. Their bodies moving in sync, Xavier lifted Monica's blouse over her head and raised her bra to expose her breasts. He placed his mouth on the left nipple and gently bit down. Monica moaned as she unbuttoned his shirt and then fumbled with the zipper of his pants. He continued to suckle her breasts. She moved her hand inside his pants and began fondling him.

"Aw, yes," he sighed as his breathing quickened. His hands were all over her body, moving slowly downward from her breasts, over her flat stomach, and on to her sex. He gently stroked the hair covering her mound before inserting two fingers inside her. She gasped and moaned as he slid them in and out, over and over.

Moaning and moving her hips, Monica was about to reach her peak. "Stop!" she whispered. "I don't want to get there yet."

"Why not?"

"I want you in me first," she said breathlessly. Xavier slid his fingers so far up inside her, one more time, that she began to quiver.

"Oh, no you don't," he said, removing his fingers completely. He laid her on the carpet and centered himself above her as she kissed his arms and lifted her hips to meet him in anticipation. He slammed himself into her and moved his hips in small circles, slowly at first and then building to bigger and faster motions.

"Yesss! I'm almost there!" she exclaimed. Xavier moved in and out of her, hard and fast, over and over again until she lost herself all over him. He thrust a few more times. His body stiffened as he released himself.

Xavier collapsed on top of her. "Ah, that was so good," he said, pulling out of her and sitting up.

"Yes, it was—so why are you getting up?" asked Monica as she kissed his back.

"I need some water. Do you want a glass?"

"Yes, I am a bit thirsty."

Xavier went to the kitchen to get the water. His thoughts returned to the botched bank robbery. So much had gone wrong. He couldn't believe how it all went down. No one was supposed to get shot—and Tremaine being on patrol at that exact time and place was just too much. He'd been trying not to think about it while he was with Monica, but he couldn't stop himself. He brought two glasses of water into the living room where Monica was laid out on the couch, watching television.

"So who are you going to the ice-cream social with?" asked Xavier. "You didn't know I would be working."

"Oh, I was just going with some of the girls from work," replied Monica. She reached for a blanket next to the couch.

"Were you even going to mention to me that you were going?"

"Well, yeah, but what's the big deal?"

"You seem like you hide things from me sometimes. I just don't like it," Xavier said.

"You disappear for days at a time when I have no idea where you are or what you're doing," Monica replied. "You could be dead for all I know. I saw Tremaine this afternoon and he said he saw you in Indianapolis when a bank robbery was going down, and then again this morning with some guy picking up a car while you drove some car that wasn't yours. What's going on, Xavier?"

"What the hell were you doing with Tremaine? Are you fucking him too? Who else are you seeing behind my back?" yelled Xavier, and he threw his glass across the room.

"I'm not seeing Tremaine or anyone else," Monica sobbed. "I saw Tremaine at the drugstore today. He gave me a ride home, is all, and he started asking me questions about you."

"I will hurt you real bad if you are ever with anyone else. You will suffer in the worst way." Xavier glared at her.

Monica was scared; she had never seen him like this. She didn't know what to do and she suddenly felt sick to her stomach. She began throwing up her dinner onto the floor in front of the couch.

"You stupid broad, you're gonna clean that up!" yelled Xavier as he stomped off to the bathroom to grab a towel. When he returned to the living room, Monica was slumped halfway on the couch and half on the floor, still vomiting. Xavier saw her and said, "Come on, I'm taking you to the hospital." He grabbed her overnight bag while she walked slowly to the car.

They arrived at the hospital and Xavier pulled up to the emergency room. Monica began throwing up again just as they reached the check-in desk. Xavier grabbed a small wastebasket and shoved it at her just in time. A nurse came around with a wheelchair while a doctor came down the hall.

"What happened to her?" the doctor asked Xavier.

"We were watching TV after dinner and she just started throwing up."

"Okay, what is her name?"

"Monica Jones."

"Hello, Monica, I'm Dr. Johnson," he said as he reached for her wrist to get a pulse. "We're going to get you into an exam room so we can see what's causing you to throw up like this. Nurse Randall will get you all set up and I'll be in shortly."

"Okay," Monica said faintly.

Another nurse asked Xavier if he was her husband, in order to obtain billing information. When Xavier told her they were not married, she directed him to the waiting room.

Meanwhile, in the exam room, the nurse asked Monica the basic medical-history questions—including if she thought she could be pregnant. Monica hesitated and then nodded yes. She then began to cry. The nurse told her everything would be fine, and she said that the doctor would be in shortly.

Oh damn, Monica thought, *I don't want to be pregnant. After today I don't even want to marry Xavier. After all these years, I've never seen him act like this before. He has always respected me. I don't know what I'm going to do.*

There was a knock on the door and the doctor entered. He talked with Monica for a moment and then performed a pelvic exam. "I do think you are pregnant, Miss Jones, but I want to draw some blood and get a urine specimen to be sure."

Monica stared at the wall above Dr. Johnson's head while he drew her blood and told her that she didn't seem to be ill. He said he would have the results of the blood work back in a few days; his nurse would call her.

"So what did they say is wrong with you?" asked Xavier once they were in the car and driving away.

"The doctor said he doesn't think I'm sick, but he thinks I am pregnant. He took my blood, did a pelvic exam, and said he would have the results back in a few days." Monica began crying again.

"Oh, shit," was all Xavier said. He drove Monica home but didn't get out of the car to walk her to the door. She grabbed her overnight bag and ran into the house. At that moment, she hated him.

The next day, Monica woke up feeling much better. She had cried herself to sleep thinking about everything that had happened the previous day. She was starting to wonder about Xavier and what he was really doing with his time. He wasn't spending much time with her, which seemed strange, especially since they were supposed to be getting married in a few weeks. At first she'd convinced herself it was because he was working so much, but now she realized she really didn't know if he even had a job. She had never been to his job, and he always changed the subject whenever she asked about it. And last night, his rudeness and threat to kill her were more than she would take. She had to call off the wedding—whether she was pregnant or not. She just couldn't marry him now that she'd seen this side of him. She was realizing what he was really capable of— just like when he threw the rock through the Andrewses' window, hurting Mrs. Andrews. Xavier had always said that was an accident, but Monica had always felt that he took a dark pleasure in knowing that his action had hurt someone.

And now, Tremaine was asking questions about Xavier and his whereabouts and the guy Xavier had been seen with. Monica had never met any of his friends outside of Marion. She thought he'd mentioned two guys who worked with him, but just in passing.

She was beginning to wonder a lot of things about Xavier. Whenever a business was robbed nearby, she realized that she and Xavier were never together on those nights. She now believed Xavier was robbing those places. But she had no proof—and after last night, she didn't want any; she feared that he meant what he'd said about killing her.

She thought about the way Xavier interacted with one of the teenage girls from the neighborhood where he grew up. Lee Ann Baldwin was her name. Monica could tell that the girl had a huge crush on him, but she didn't know the extent of it, so she never brought it up. All she knew was that Xavier seemed to encourage the girl's flirtations.

Monica was just getting out of bed when her phone began to ring. She didn't want to answer it in case it was Xavier. She needed some time away from him, to get her head and emotions wrapped around what was happening. But it could be one of the girls from work. "Hello?" she answered.

"Hey, baby." It was Xavier. "I'm sorry I was acting weird with you last night. Why don't you wait for me to get off work today and we can go to the ice-cream social together?"

"No, I already told you, I'm going with a couple of girls from work." She cringed as she spoke to him.

"I really want to take you, to make up for last night," Xavier persisted. "I didn't treat you right at all, even when you told me you might be pregnant."

"Yeah, you were an asshole, and I hate you for that. I don't want to see you today because you hurt me in a way I never thought you would."

"That's not fair, Monica. I said I was sorry and I want to make it up to you," he pleaded.

"Why don't we just meet up after the ice-cream social if I'm feeling okay?"

"Yeah, we'll meet up—and you better not be with Tremaine, either, like I told you yesterday." Xavier hung up the phone.

For a few minutes Monica stood, shaking with fear, the phone still in her hand.

Monica went to the ice-cream social with her friends. It was held in the large parking lot shared by the soda shop and the town hardware store. It seemed like half the town had shown up. Picnic tables were set up with bright red tablecloths. In the center of each table sat a vase filled with beautiful orange, yellow, pink, and white flowers. Three tables had been set up in front of the soda shop, with huge containers of ice cream and big, colorful balloons. Monica was enjoying herself being out with the girls. She'd been attending these socials with her mom ever since she was a little girl.

At three o'clock, the time Xavier had said he'd be getting off work, Monica began to feel nervous. She hadn't told him that she was attending with Tracey and Stacey, Tremaine's twin sisters, in addition to some of the other girls she worked with. The girls had found a table under some trees at the edge of the parking lot. From there Monica could see everyone coming and going. She hoped Tremaine wouldn't show up, because she didn't want Xavier acting jealous and threatening her again.

"So are you getting nervous about the wedding?" asked Stacey.

"Uh, yeah," replied Monica. She hadn't told them about the way Xavier had been acting or of his threats last night and again today.

"Are you okay?" Tracey asked. "You don't seem yourself today."

"I'm fine, just getting butterflies, I guess," she replied with a slight smile.

"Let us know if there's anything we can do to help you out. We can't have our girl all crazy over this wedding," said Felicia, one of her coworkers.

"Yes, we're here for you!" offered another girl.

"Thank you. I will let you know—you're all too sweet."

Suddenly Stacey said, "Look, Tracey, Daddy and Tremaine are here. I don't see Mom with them—and why are they in their uniforms?"

"I don't know, but I'm sure we'll find out soon. Here they come."

"Hello, ladies," said Assistant Chief Wilbur Tillman.

"Hi," they all said in unison.

"Monica, have you seen Xavier today?" asked Tremaine.

"No, he said he was coming here after he gets off work," she replied. "Why, Tremaine? What's going on?"

"Come walk with me, Monica," Wilbur gently insisted. Monica nodded as she stood to go with the assistant police chief.

After walking several yards away from the crowd, Assistant Chief Tillman asked, "Monica, what do you know about Xavier's employment at Buehler's Corporation?"

"Only that he says he's been working there for a couple of years. You don't think he really works there, do you?"

"No, I don't. In fact, I called the place and they do not have him as an employee there and never have. Do you know where he was the past few days?"

"No, he told me he was at work. If he doesn't work there, I don't know where he was. Tremaine told me he saw him a couple nights ago in Indianapolis, and again yesterday morning. Tremaine knows more about the whereabouts of my fiancé than I do. What is it you think he's done?"

"Have you heard of the robberies here in Marion, or Anderson, Gas City, and Muncie, and the bank robbery in Indianapolis a couple of nights ago? We have reason to believe Xavier was involved. Do you remember if you were with him on the night of any of these robberies?"

"I don't know for sure, but I was thinking how odd it is when he disappears for days at a time. No phone calls or anything. He may be seeing another woman, though. I just don't know, Chief. But I am ready to call off the wedding."

"I understand how upsetting this is for you. We're going to take Xavier in today for some questioning. Do you think he'll show up here?"

"I don't know. He could be somewhere watching me at this moment, if what you say is true about his not having a job."

"I want you to go back over to the girls and act like nothing is up. And do not leave with him if he shows up. We will take him in. I'm hoping he comes willingly."

"Okay, I can do this," Monica said. Her voice cracked and her hands were shaking. She drew a deep breath.

"You'll be fine no matter what happens," Wilbur reassured her.

Monica walked back to her friends at the table. "Does anyone want to get some ice cream?"

"Yeah!" a couple of the girls replied as they stood up.

"Is everything okay, Monica?" Tracey asked.

"Yes, they just need to talk to Xavier about something," replied Monica. "Everything's fine, though."

They were in line for ice cream when Xavier grabbed Monica from behind. "Hello, Monica," he said.

"Hi," she replied as she turned around to face him. She glanced around to see where Chief Tillman and Tremaine were. She spotted them in different areas of the parking lot, engaged in conversations—but she saw them noticing Xavier's arrival.

They didn't approach him right away; they let him enjoy the event for a while. They wanted to wait until the crowd thinned, in case Xavier decided he wasn't going with them. He didn't act as if he knew they were watching him.

Monica clenched her hands to avoid trembling. "How was work?"

Xavier shrugged. "Work was work."

"I'm glad you could make it." Her voice cracked a bit on the lie. She hoped he hadn't noticed.

"Of course I made it. I had to check up on you, didn't I? You know, see who you're fucking."

Monica took a step back. "I don't have to put up with this shit." She turned to walk away.

Xavier grabbed her arm. "You'll put up with whatever I tell you, you crazy bitch."

"*You're* crazy. I don't know what's gotten into you, but you're scaring me," she said as she pulled away from him.

"Good, you should be scared!" he yelled as he drew back his fist and punched her in the face.

Monica grabbed her face and screamed, "You stupid bastard!" Just as Xavier was going to punch her again, Tremaine grabbed his wrist and tackled him. Monica had seen Tremaine coming and had moved out of the way just in time.

"You are under arrest," Tremaine told him. Assistant Chief Tillman took over the arrest since Tremaine was out of jurisdiction. Wilbur handcuffed Xavier and walked him to the squad car. Tracey, Stacey, and several of their friends looked after Monica. Her cheek was already beginning to bruise and swell where Xavier had struck her.

Tremaine began asking people in the crowd what they had seen. He wanted to get statements before anyone left. Deputies from the Marion police force showed a few minutes later. Chief Tillman had them on standby in case Xavier tried to run. A rookie deputy asked Monica if she would come down to the station to make a complaint against Xavier. She agreed to, so he drove her there after they had all of the witnesses' information. He then took her to the hospital to make sure she was okay and didn't have any broken bones in her cheek or jaw.

—— ◆ ——

The cruiser hummed along the deserted highway at a good clip. Xavier figured they must be doing eighty. Sheriff Hale and his two stooges hadn't said a word to him since they'd released him from jail. Xavier leaned forward. "Where're you taking me? You can't hold me. You ain't got nothing on me. Nothing."

Hale ignored him. Instead, he turned to a deputy and asked, "You think Johnny U. still has it in him?" The deputy grunted. Neither man even glanced at Xavier.

Xavier sat back in a huff. He balled a fist and pounded it into his seat. The men continued to ignore him.

Screw these guys. I've served my time. Chumps can't do nothing. He tried to relax and watch out the window. The car sped past a mileage sign for Chicago. Chicago might be good. He could lay low there. Big city like that, it would be easy to disappear. People there treat you with respect. Not like these local yokels.

A sign along the road grew larger, welcoming them to Wabash. What the hell were these assholes up to? They drove past a cornfield that was acres long and wide. They stopped on the side of the road, pulled Xavier out of the car, and made him walk into the field with them. They came upon an opening in the field; it was clear of anything for about twenty yards in circumference.

"What the hell is this? What are you doing?" asked Xavier.

"You see all this hidden land? And did you know the surrounding corn drowns out any noises?" asked one of the deputies.

"Why are you fucking showing me this shit? If you're gonna kill me, just do it and get it over with," Xavier shouted.

"Oh, we're not going to kill you—but *they* will if you don't leave Indiana now and don't ever step foot in this state again. Come on out, boys!" Sheriff Hale yelled in Xavier's face. Twenty or more men stepped out of the stalks of corn carrying guns and large farm tools. They were all dressed in white sheets and had hoods covering their faces. They were the Ku Klux Klan.

PART 2

SHANNON

CHAPTER 9

Shannon Wilson was born in Marion, Indiana, on February 4, 1956, to Lionel and Andrea Wilson. She was the ninth of sixteen children. Mrs. Wilson had five sisters and two brothers; Mr. Wilson had one sister and five brothers. So Shannon had many cousins in Marion—some of whom were double cousins—and even more relatives throughout the Midwest and across the nation.

The older children in the family were responsible for the younger kids. Each older child got to pick which younger sibling they'd take care of for the day. Shannon's sister Charlotte often chose to take care of her. Shannon was a quiet child who enjoyed spending time with her family and friends.

When Shannon was about four or five years old, Marion had a bad flood. Floods were nothing new to the town, but this one was by far the worst anyone could remember. The family lost a lot of their belongings and had to make do with what they had left. The girls made paper baby dolls and clothes for the few dolls that remained. This is how they learned to improvise, to make the most out of the little they had.

As Shannon became a teenager, she liked to hang out with her cousins and friends from school. When they had extra money, they enjoyed roller-skating, shopping, and going to the movies. Sometimes they would go to the parks, or just listen to music at the soda shop. Most of all they went to house parties. The parties were usually free—sometimes they would cost a dollar—and everyone always had a lot of fun.

Shannon also had a love for fashion that was beyond that of the typical teenage girl. In her early teens she would babysit, run errands, and do odd jobs to earn money. She wanted to have nice things, especially clothes and jewelry. Sometimes she hung around people who would loot clothes from the stores; she bought the clothes from them for cheap. A lot of the teens were doing that to get things they needed; they considered it their way of earning a living.

Most people really liked Shannon and enjoyed being around her. She was pleasant and funny, and she liked to joke around. Sometimes friends and family couldn't tell when she was joking and when she was serious.

One evening after a big snowfall, when Shannon was about fourteen, she and some of her cousins were outside playing in front of her house. Her younger cousin Jay said, "Hey, I bet you can't hit the next car that drives by with a snowball."

"I know I can hit it!" shouted her little brother Jacob. They all got their snowballs ready for when the next car drove by. They threw snowballs as the car drove past.

"That was so fun!" Shannon said. Everyone was laughing and enjoying the excitement of the fresh snow. Some of their snowballs rolled into a puddle, so Jay and Jacob grabbed them and waited to throw them at the next vehicle.

Bam! Bam! The thud of the snowballs hitting the cars was much louder than the previous ones had been. These sounded almost like rocks.

"What did you guys throw at that car?" Shannon asked Jay and Jacob.

"Our snowballs rolled into a puddle and they kind of got icy," explained Jay. "That was so loud!"

"Yeah, let's get all our snowballs wet and throw them at the next car!" Jacob said.

"No, we could put dents in the cars," said Shannon.

"But it's funny how loud it is, and the people's reaction," Jay argued.

"Okay," Shannon relented, "but just this once."

All of the kids made their snowballs and put them in the puddles of water for a few minutes. When they each had two icy snowballs, they hid behind some bushes and waited until another vehicle came by. Shannon wasn't standing behind the bushes far enough when a car came by and suddenly stopped. It was a lady from her church. She rolled down her window.

"Shannon, I thought that was you. Child, what are you doing out here?"

"I was just visiting with some friends. They, um, had to leave," she said, stumbling over her words.

"Well, go on and get in the house, it's starting to get dark."

"Yes, ma'am." *I probably should go in; I am getting kind of cold. But this is so fun.*

After about ten minutes, another car came down the street toward them. They waited until the car was almost right in front of them. *Boom, boom! Boom, boom, boom!*

Screech! The car stopped and a burly black man jumped out of the car. "I'm gonna beat all y'all little bastards' asses!" he yelled as all the kids ran and hid.

Mrs. Wilson came to the front door when she heard the yelling; she saw the man turn and get back in his car. After he drove away, she called for the kids to come in. The kids came out from hiding and went to the front door where Mrs. Wilson was standing. "Why was that man yelling and who was he yelling at?" she demanded.

"We don't know," said Jacob. "We were in the back."

"Yeah," agreed Jay and some of the other kids from the neighborhood.

"No you weren't. I heard you all out front here, and then the man was yelling something. I want the truth."

"Okay, Mamma," said Shannon. "He was yelling at us because we were throwing snowballs at cars as they drove past." She didn't mention that they were ice balls.

"Shannon and Jacob, get in the house. The rest of you go home. Jay, Victoria, Marie, you go straight home. I'm calling my sister right now to let her know what you all did. Do you hear me?"

"Yes, ma'am," they mumbled with their heads hung down as they turned to walk away.

"Damn, Jay," Victoria complained, "you just had to start throwing the ice balls, now we all gonna get in trouble."

"You did it, too! You didn't have to throw them! Don't blame me because your stupid tail thought it was funny too!" yelled Jay.

"Well, you're going in the house first," Marie said. "You know she's gonna have the switches waiting, and even if I hadn't thrown the ice balls, we'd still get in trouble for being with you."

Meanwhile, back at the Wilson home, Mrs. Wilson had punished Jacob and Shannon with her own switches. She was still speaking with Shannon about how easy it was for people to manipulate her into doing things she knew she ain't got no business doing.

"Girl, why don't you think for yourself and stick up for what you know is right? I expect so much more out of you than the younger kids. You are older than the rest of the kids who were with you— and yet you let them talk you into thinking it was right to damage people's cars. You have got to think for yourself and make better choices. Do you understand?"

"Yes, ma'am. I was just having fun with them. I even told them no at first because we could dent the cars," Shannon said.

"That's what you were supposed to do—but then you gave in instead of coming and telling me," said Mrs. Wilson. "You have got to think for yourself, child."

Jehovah, please let my baby learn to think for herself and make wiser decisions as she goes through life. Mrs. Wilson prayed hard for her ninth child.

CHAPTER 10

When Shannon was fourteen, she discovered she was good at telling jokes. She loved to play harmless pranks on people. No one ever knew whether she was playing around or serious. She especially liked to sneak up on her family and friends to scare them. When her mom or one of her sisters would be cooking or washing dishes, she would walk up quietly and just stand there behind them. One time Shannon did that to her sister Charlotte while she was cooking. Charlotte screamed and jumped, and then she yelled, "I'ma tell Ma!"

Shannon laughed. "I'm sorry—I couldn't help but scare you! You were in your own little world, cooking and humming along. You should have seen yourself! Girl, you looked like you saw a ghost—and I swear you jumped three feet off the ground."

"You're gonna give someone a heart attack one day, you keep scaring people like that. It's not funny, either. I'm gonna kick your ass if you scare me again," complained Charlotte. "In fact, you get in here and help me finish cooking. And you can do the dishes afterward too."

"But Char, I said I was sorry!"

"You don't act sorry, because you keep scaring people on purpose all the time. And you always laugh about it."

"I will try not to scare you anymore. But you have to admit it's funny seeing people get so scared." Shannon laughed.

"Girl, you're so silly. Let's finish this dinner before Mamma comes in here." They continued making the dinner of cabbage, fried chicken, and cornbread. They talked and joked around until it was time to eat. Shannon refrained from scaring her family for a while.

One day, Shannon was out walking with some friends from school and her cousin Paula. "I'm bored," Shannon said. "Let's do something."

"Like what?" asked Paula.

They were nearing their friend Tonya's house. "Tonya said she would be babysitting because her mom was going somewhere," said Shannon.

"Okay, so let's go over her house for a while," said Frankie B.

"Wait," Shannon said, "I want to scare her. Go to your house and get one of your mom's wigs and a pair of stockings."

"Okay, but what are you gonna do?" Frankie B. asked.

"You'll see; just go get the stuff for me."

Frankie ran down the street and around the block. He lived close to Tonya, so it wouldn't take him long.

Shannon had known Frankie B. since they were in elementary school; he was a couple of years older than her. She had a huge crush on him—and he knew it and liked her too. They always had fun together and got along well. They had a good friendship.

"Here you go," said Frankie, handing the items to Shannon. She laughed as she put the stockings over her head and pulled them down over her face. She put the wig on and began heading to Tonya's house. She snuck up to the living-room window, where she could see Tonya sitting with her brothers and sisters watching television. Shannon waved to the others to come closer, putting a finger to her lips. When they were close enough to be seen, Shannon banged her fist on the window and yelled, "Boo!"

Tonya and her siblings screamed at the top of their lungs. Shannon saw Tonya's mom come running into the living room. *Shit, her mom's still home!*

The older woman went to the front door and yelled at the kids outside, "You little bastards go home and don't come back!"

Shannon and her friends took off running and laughing. When they reached the next block, they stopped—but they were still laughing hard. "Did you see them all screaming for dear life!" said Shannon, taking off the wig and stockings. "And her mom was still home! That was so much fun!"

"Shannon, you're crazy!" Pamela said. "I can't believe you did that. The wig and stockings over your face were too much!"

"Yeah," the others joined in. "That was really funny!"

They continued walking around for a little while longer. Shannon and Frankie B. walked everyone else home, and then Frankie walked Shannon home. As they walked, Frankie said, "You sure do like to have fun and take risks."

"I do like having fun, but I'm not so risky. I didn't think about Tonya's mom knowing it was me and telling my ma. I was just thinking about the fun."

"Well, you gave us all a good laugh tonight. That's one of the things I like about you." Frankie took hold of Shannon's hand. They walked the rest of the way in silence. When they reached Shannon's house, Frankie leaned in and gave her a long, lingering kiss. She was breathless and didn't want the kiss to end.

They pulled apart when two of Shannon's older brothers came walking out the front door. "Hey, Shannon. Hey, Frankie B.," said Adrian.

"Hi," they said in unison.

"Don't even think about it, Frankie," said John as he playfully punched Frankie in the arm.

Shannon blushed. "Damn, John, stop playing around," she said, nudging her brother down the steps.

"I'm serious," John said with a smirk.

"What are you talking about?" Frankie laughed.

"I think you know exactly what I'm talking about," teased John.

The guys all laughed. Adrian and John went on their way. Shannon looked horrified at first, but once her brothers were out of sight, she reached up and held Frankie's face in her hands. She lifted her lips slightly as she pulled his mouth to hers, kissing him hard and passionately.

After a while she pulled her mouth away. "Um, we better stop before anyone else comes out here."

"Dang, I was really enjoying your soft lips. Look at what you do to me," he sighed, looking down at his nature.

"Good night, Frankie," she said, blushing, and went into the house.

That night as she lay in bed, Shannon thought about how much she really did like Frankie B. She dreamed about them being married and having a family when they got older.

Shannon and Frankie continued to hang out together. They would go to the movies and shopping. He took her roller-skating and to the county fair when it came to town.

One Saturday afternoon, Jay came over to play with Jacob. "Hi, Jay," she said. "Are you going skating tomorrow?"

"Yeah, after I go to church in the morning. You know Mother won't let us go skating or anywhere else if we don't go to church Sunday morning. And I need to find a ride."

"I'm going with Frankie B.; you can ride with us. Jacob, you could come along too."

"Okay!" both boys replied.

At church on Sunday morning, while Jay was singing in the choir, he was thinking, *I hope Reverend don't get long-winded with the sermon like he usually does.* At that moment he heard Sonny start shouting, as he did every Sunday. Sonny always shouted and danced in the pews. Some said he had the Holy Ghost, but Jay thought it was all an act.

Jay whispered to another choir member, "I'll give him five minutes before he hits the floor!" Sure enough, no more than three minutes passed and Sonny was jerking and running up and down the pew aisles, shouting and praising God. Jay and his friends in the choir began snickering. Gwen, the choir director, gave them all a stern look, telling them they had better stop laughing and straighten up.

As the service continued, Jay started wondering where he'd put his skates. *Man, I can't wear those beat-up skates they have at the skating rink. Oh yeah, they're under the bed. I sure hope they hurry up with the service.* Jay loved going skating and his cousin knew it. Shannon loved bringing happiness to her friends and family.

When Jay finally got home from church, he quickly starch-ironed his jeans and cleaned up his skates. Just as he finished, he heard a car horn. He opened the front door to see Frankie B. and Shannon. Jacob was in the back seat. "Hey," he said, "Victoria wants to come; do you have enough room for her?"

"Sure, there's room for one more," said Frankie B.

"Tell her to come on, but she better be quiet—we all know how she likes to run her mouth!" Shannon laughed.

The Midway Skating Rink was about five miles north of downtown, in the more rural part of Marion. It was an old barn that had been converted into a rink.

Jay and Frankie B. had brought their own skates; the others went to rent theirs. They got on the floor just in time for the warm-up. After that they heard trumpets and then "Get up and dance to the music!" *Doom, doom, da doom doom, doom.* "Dance to the music!" Everyone rushed to the floor to skate to the 1968 hit "Dance to the Music" by Sly and the Family Stone.

"Make sure you keep up!" Shannon shouted over the music as she skated off ahead of the others. Jay had just joined the crowd skating around the edge of the rink when he noticed some people skating in the middle of the floor. *That looks fun!* he thought. He decided to try it. As he was approaching the center, his eyes got wide; the other skaters were moving so fast around the circle. *Shoot, I need to do something,* Jay thought.

All of a sudden, Frankie B. grabbed Jay and picked him up, skating through the traffic. "Hey, little man, you have to know what you're doing when you go through the middle. Next time around just follow me," Frankie B. instructed.

"Okay!" said Jay, following behind Frankie B. They went through the middle a few times; Jay had a blast.

A slow song came on next, so Jay and Jacob left the floor. He watched Shannon and Frankie B. skate to "Everybody Plays a Fool" by the Main Ingredient. He noticed his sister Victoria skating with some boy he'd seen around but didn't know.

All of a sudden Jay heard a lot of commotion. People were arguing; it sounded like a fight was about to break out. Frankie, Victoria, and Shannon skated up to the boys. "Take your skates off and grab your shoes. It's time to go."

They hurried to get into the car, and Frankie took off. "I'm glad we got out of there fast," Victoria said. "Those fools were acting crazy."

"Yeah, but I did want to see a good fight," said Shannon.

"I think they were going to do more than fight," said Frankie B. "I know some of those guys, and they don't fight, they shoot! I had to get y'all out of there—I'm not having none of y'all's folks coming after me." Frankie shifted into fourth gear and floored it.

"Hey, Frankie, here comes everyone," said Victoria, looking back. All the cars were racing back to Marion.

"Yeah, I see them in the mirror." Frankie watched his speed climb to a hundred miles per hour.

"Wow, we're really rolling now!" squealed Shannon. "This is fun."

"Hold on, I'm going to pass this car so I can go even faster."

"Look, one more—you might as well pass them all," said Victoria.

"Yeah, I will." Frankie pushed the old DeSoto to 120 miles per hour. He looked up to see that the driver of the one car remaining in front of him had hit its brakes. From the right-hand lane, the other car gradually began to turn in front of them, into the left lane. Frankie said, "Do you see that? I think he's trying to turn around in the middle of the street!" Sure enough, the car ahead was now blocking both lanes of traffic. Frankie had nowhere to go. There were ditches on both sides of the road; if he swerved into them at the speed he was going, the car would surely flip over.

"Hold on, everyone!" Frankie yelled as he slammed on his brakes. The car screeched loudly, and then *bam*! Metal to metal, with the loudest screeching sound they'd ever heard, their car slammed into the rear driver's side of the other car. Frankie felt the steering wheel hit his chest. Shannon's drink spilled all over the front seat, and everyone in the backseat flew forward into the back of the seats in front of them.

When everything had stopped moving, Shannon asked, "Frankie, are you okay, baby?"

"Yeah. Let's get out of the car." But Frankie realized that the steering wheel was tight against his chest, pinning him into the seat. He had to squirm and wiggle his way out of the car. Once everyone was free of both cars, Frankie looked over to the other vehicle and saw his cousin Tommy.

Shannon ran up to Tommy. "What the hell were you doing? Are you crazy?" she yelled. "You know everyone races back from skating, Tommy!"

Tommy was shaking. He stuttered, "Suh-suh-someone forgot something so-so-so I had to go back."

"Well, it must have been really important." Frankie B. grabbed Shannon and whispered, "Come on, Shannon, you know Tommy's a little off in the head."

"I don't care. He almost killed us all. We have my young cousins and little brother with us—what if something had happened to them!"

"Look, bitch, it was an accident." One of Tommy's passengers had climbed out of the vehicle and was looking at the damage.

"Yeah, well, that crazy motherfucker could have killed us all. We need to call the police."

"We ain't calling no police," said Tommy's passenger, flashing a gun in his waistband and closing his distance on Shannon.

"Whoa," said Frankie B., "we don't want no trouble, just leave. We won't call the police."

"You better not," the passenger said, grabbing the butt of the gun for emphasis. The gunman was Xavier Hudson.

CHAPTER 11

Shannon went to school each day and made average grades. She had to help care for some of her younger siblings, although they were not much younger than she was. The youngest was only seven years behind her.

Shannon and Frankie B. officially began dating each other shortly after she turned fifteen. They went to many house parties together; sometimes they would meet there. After dancing and partying with their friends, they'd often find a nice dark corner where they could kiss and fondle each other.

Shannon had decided for herself that she was ready to go all the way with Frankie B. She had been thinking about it a lot, going back and forth about whether to remain a virgin. They had been dating and spending a lot of time together—and she loved him. They had done everything but have sex. She was scared, since she'd never done it before, and she wasn't on any birth control. *But if I don't do it with him, he'll do it with someone else.* Shannon thought about recent conversations with her friends. "Girl, you need to go ahead and give him some. He so cute—if you don't let him, I will!" Her friend laughed as she gyrated her hips.

One Friday night, Frankie B. and Shannon met up at a house party, at the home of one of Frankie B.'s classmates. Shannon and her friends arrived before Frankie and his friends. They heard the bass blasting from speakers when they were still halfway down the block. People were partying outside in the driveway, to the side of the house, and toward a door farther back.

After Shannon and her friends made their way to the side door and paid their dollar each, they went down some stairs where the music was even louder. It was dark, with spots of glowing blue and red from lamps around the room. At a card table in the farthest corner of the room, an older dude and chick sold cheap liquor, beer, and sodas. Everyone was dancing, trying to talk above the music, having a good time.

Shannon's thoughts drifted to Frankie B. as she stood against a wall listening to a slow, romantic song. *I am going to do it with him tonight, if we can find some time alone. Why should I let some other girl sex up my boyfriend? I can do it myself. Besides, I love him, so it's okay to have sex with him.*

"Shannon, look who's here," said her friend. "You really need to go get that bitch off your man!"

Shannon looked to where her friend was pointing. Some girl from school was hanging all over Frankie B. She went over to them and said, "What the hell is going on?"

"Baby, I just got here and this bitch starts hugging on me. I don't even know her."

Shannon pushed the girl off Frankie. "Bitch, if you ever touch my boyfriend again, I will beat your ass!"

"Whoa, Shannon! She's just drunk. It doesn't mean anything. Come on," Frankie said pulling her away from the drunk girl. He found a quiet corner in a small bedbroom just off the main room. He pulled her close to him and hugged her. "Hey, are you okay?"

"Yes, but that chick best stay away from you. You really don't know her?" Shannon asked.

"No, I don't. Me and some of the guys just got here and came downstairs. All of a sudden she grabbed me and wouldn't stop hugging on me. She thought I was someone else." He bent to kiss her.

"Okay," she said, kissing him back. She could taste the alcohol on his breath. They talked for a while before noticing no one else was in the room anymore. They began making out. He was feeling her entire body; she responded with moans and moved her pelvis against him. He kissed her neck and rubbed her breasts. The material of her shirt became taut across her nipples. She kissed him back as he pushed his tongue in her mouth and swirled it around her own tongue.

"We better stop," Frankie B. said, pulling away from her.

She grabbed his arm. "No, I don't want to stop."

"Are you sure?" He went to the door and locked it.

"Um, yes. Just make sure you pull out."

"Okay." Frankie B. shut and locked the bedroom door.

He began unbuttoning her blouse and slid it off her shoulders. "Good gracious! You are so beautiful." He lifted her bra, exposing her breasts, and he bent down and kissed each one.

"Oh, that's nice," she moaned. "Let's lie down." She sat on the floor and pulled him to her.

He lay on top of her, and they kissed some more. "Oh, baby, I want you so bad," he said. He unbuttoned her pants and pulled at the zipper. She raised her hips as he pulled her pants and panties down and off her ankles. He kissed her spot.

"Are you sure you want to do this?" he asked as he slid his body upon hers.

"Please be gentle. I'm scared," she said into his mouth as he kissed her.

"I will." He took his pants off in record time and lay back down on top of her. He slowly eased himself into her.

"Ouch, it hurts."

"It will for a little bit, but then it'll feel good." He eased himself in and out of her, careful not to go to too deep too quickly. After a while she began to raise her hips to meet his with each thrust.

"Ah, that feels so good," she said.

"It sure does. You ready to let me bust it all the way?"

"Yes." She braced her hand against his body as he thrust forward hard, and she felt a sharp pain.

"*Ow*, it hurts—but it feels good at the same time."

"Yeah, baby, and you so wet and ready for me." He moved himself in and out of her, over and over, careful not to pull himself out all the way. "Ah, that's good, baby. I'm going to bust." Frankie moved faster and deeper until his body stiffened and he reached his climax.

Shannon felt a pulling in her stomach, taking her to a place she hadn't known about. "Ah, that feels so good. Don't stop, baby, yes!" She felt she couldn't breathe as Frankie collapsed on top of her. *Damn, he forgot to pull out. Can I get pregnant on the first time?*

"Damn, girl, that was so good."

"I felt funny at first, but then it got so good, I couldn't stop. You didn't stop either."

"It felt too good. I forgot all about stopping in time. I just busted all inside you. It should be okay since it was your first time, right?" Frankie B. asked as they put their clothes back on.

"How would I know? We better get back to the party." *I can't believe he just forgot to pull out of me. I don't want a baby yet. Damn him!*

At another party the following weekend, they were talking with friends and dancing, just having a good time. They found a quiet corner where they could talk for a while. Frankie B. had been drinking a bit; he was sweet-talking Shannon and kissing her on the neck. He led her to a dark back room where boxes and musty blankets were stored. Shannon kissed Frankie B. deep and fully. She planted wet kisses on his cheeks and neck.

"I want to do it to you so badly," Frankie said.

"I want you too, Frankie." They kissed and caressed each other, falling to the floor and having a quick sexual encounter as the music played and friends danced and partied down the hall.

"Damn, that felt good," Shannon said breathlessly. "But you forgot to pull out again! I better not get pregnant."

"That was real good, and you won't get pregnant," said Frankie B. as they pulled up their pants. "I hope. I tried to pull out, but I just couldn't help myself. It felt way too good."

"Okay, let's sneak back out to the party." Shannon pulled her pants up and tucked in her shirt. She fixed her hair and led Frankie

B. by the hand out of the room and onto the dance floor. They danced to a couple of slow songs and then grabbed a couple drinks.

"I love hanging out with you—you always know how to have a fun time," said Frankie as he grabbed her by the waist from behind and kissed her cheek. Shannon pulled his arms tight around her and smiled up at him.

At that moment, Shannon's cousins Paula and Marcia walked up to them. "So where have you two been?" asked Paula with a smile. She and Marcia had watched them come out of the back room and blend in with the other teens on the dance floor.

"Uh, we were in the back, talking," replied Shannon.

"Yeah, not so much noise back there," Frankie added.

"I bet it's nice and quiet in that back room," laughed Paula.

"We saw you sneaking out," added Marcia. "Hmm, I wonder what you were really doing in there?"

"We, um, okay. We were fooling around," blurted Shannon under the knowing stares of her cousins.

"Uh-huh, I knew y'all have been doing the nasty!" exclaimed Marcia.

"Ooh, girl," Paula whispered to Shannon, "you better not get pregnant, Auntie will have a fit!"

"Yeah, I know she wouldn't be happy with me. But girl, I can't help myself when it comes to Frankie!"

"I know—trust me, I do understand how you feel about him. I feel the same way about Andre," said Paula. "But you have to be careful and make sure you protect yourself. Let's talk about all that later. I feel like dancing some more, but I need to go outside and smoke."

"Okay, I'll go with you. And I got a couple of joints from Frankie B. Ain't nothing like a good joint and a cigarette," said Shannon. The three girls wove their way through the crowd of people dancing and standing around talking, until they reached the back door. They stood outside talking as they passed the joint back and forth.

"I can't wait until spring break," said Marcia.

"Girl," Shannon replied, "you're always ready for a break from school. It will be nice, though. I don't really like going to school either."

"You all best enjoy it while you can," Paula said, "After watching Mother go to work every day and come home tired all the time, I don't know which is worse—going to school or going to work."

Shannon said, "I'm not gonna work that hard. I hope Frankie's gonna take care of me! I want nice clothes, lots of jewelry, and a nice place to live with the best furniture and fur rugs."

"You're crazy," Paula said with disgust. "Frankie's a drug dealer. What kind of life would you have? Always having drug addicts around you, never knowing when one would try to harm you, or other dealers hurting you to get to Frankie. God forbid if you have children, they would target them too."

"He's not a drug dealer. He just dabbles in selling a little weed here and there. Besides, he's getting a good job in Nap after he graduates. I won't even have to work unless I want to. Think of all the clothes I can have and won't have to have them boosted. And besides, Frankie wouldn't let anything happen to me or our kids."

"You can believe that if you want to. He can't be with you every minute—and he can't protect you from a bullet," argued Paula.

"I know that, but I'd be able to protect myself, too," replied Shannon. "Besides, that's a long time from now. Let's go back in and party!"

The girls went back in the house and partied until it was over. Frankie B. had left the party when they'd gone out to smoke, but he came back to give them rides home. He dropped off Paula and Marcia first, and then took Shannon home. He walked her to her front door and kissed her goodnight.

"Will I see you tomorrow?" Shannon asked him.

"I don't know, I have a lot of runs to make and probably won't get done until late. I'll try to call you, though." Shannon pouted, so Frankie pulled her close in his arms and gave her another kiss. "Don't be like that, baby. You know I have to make money, and Fridays and

Saturdays are my busiest days. Besides, I'll make it up to you on Sunday."

"How? What are we going to do?"

"I don't know, but make sure you can get away for most of the day, okay?"

"Yeah, sure. Make sure you call me tomorrow, though," Shannon demanded.

"All right, I will, I will," said Frankie.

Nine months later, Shannon and Frankie B. had a baby girl. They named her Teresa. She was a beautiful baby who looked just like Frankie. Four years later, they had another baby: a little boy they named Lamont.

Shannon lived at home with her parents until 1974, when she graduated from high school and got a job at the factory of the Radio Corporation of America. Her cousins Colette and Paula also worked at RCA, along with many people she knew from Marion and surrounding towns. The factory, which mainly manufactured televisions and inexpensive stereos, shut down each summer for two weeks. During the shutdown, Shannon and Paula would sometimes visit Shannon's older siblings who'd moved to Minneapolis. They enjoyed going to the free concerts in the parks and at the lakes.

CHAPTER 12

One night in 1977, after a few drinks at Tiny's Bar with friends from work, Paula and Shannon were walking to Paula's car when they saw someone sitting on the hood.

"What the hell are you doing sitting on my damn car?" asked Paula before she saw who it was.

"Aw, damn," mumbled Shannon as she looked up to see Frankie B. sitting on her cousin's car. *This is gonna get ugly,* she thought, noticing the smug smile on Frankie's face. Shannon approached the car. Frankie smiled at her. His bloodshot eyes were only half-open, but even at that she could see his dilated pupils. Shit, he was stoned, and the smell of Old Grand-Dad clung to him like the world's worst cologne.

"Who do you think you're talking to?" slurred Frankie B.

"You, fool! Now get the hell off my car."

"I don't know why you're getting all upset over this raggedy-ass piece of car," said Frankie, laughing. She was right in his face now and wasn't backing down.

"Paula, let's just go," Shannon pleaded.

"Yeah, bitch, get away from me before I smack the shit out of you!" warned Frankie.

"You put your damn hands on me and you're gonna be real sorry. Now get your ass off my car, damn it!" As soon as Paula's words were out, Frankie swung back and slapped Paula hard across her face; it stung and she could feel her face begin to swell as welts started to appear across her cheek.

"Oh, you no-good bastard! I got something fo' your ass!" she screamed as she got into her car and Shannon jumped in the passenger side. Paula had already planned what she would do. She was going home to get a gun one of her brothers had given her months earlier.

"I'll be right back, Shannon. I gotta go take care of something."

"Don't go doing something crazy. What are you going to do?"

"I'm going to get my gun!"

"Girl, don't do that. You want to end up in jail over *this*?"

"I have to. He's not getting away with slapping me like that!"

"Damn, I can't believe he slapped you like that. He can be a real asshole when he's drinking. But you have to think of your daughter. He's not worth it."

"I'm gonna get his ass. I got to go. If I'm not back in fifteen minutes, get a ride from someone."

"Okay, but don't you want me to come with you?" asked Shannon.

"No, I'll be all right. I just need to go now," Paula said.

Shannon got out of the car and glared at Frankie as she walked over to her other friends. They stood outside talking about what had happened while they waited for Paula to come back. Shannon was about to leave with Jessie and Jocelyn when she spotted Paula, turning into the parking lot so fast her tires squealed. She pulled up right next to Frankie B. Paula jumped out of her car, leaving the engine idling, and pulled the gun out of her purse. Her hands were shaking as she thought about what she was doing. *I'll just shoot him in his foot—even though I should blow his damn balls off.*

"Don't shoot," Frankie pleaded, throwing his hands in the air. She aimed the gun at his privates. She could hear Shannon yelling at her to stop.

Paula quickly lowered the gun so it was aiming directly at his left foot and shot at Frankie B. The first bullet hit the side of his car as the gun jerked upward, so she quickly fired off another shot, a direct hit to the side of his left foot. People screamed and ran, trying to dodge any bullets if she decided to keep shooting.

"Aw, shit!" Frankie B. screamed in pain; dark blood began seeping through his shoe. He opened the door to his car and hopped in the backseat while one of his friends got in the driver's seat. Paula jumped back in her own car and Shannon got into the passenger side. Paula threw it in reverse and sped out of the parking lot before Shannon could shut her door.

"Oh shit, I can't believe I just shot his ass," Paula said as she sped off.

"Girl, are you fucking crazy? What the hell were you thinking?" asked Shannon.

"I don't know, he just pissed me off when he slapped me. I had to show him he couldn't get away with that shit!" exclaimed Paula.

"We've gotta get out of Marion. I don't want to stay here," Shannon said when Paula got to her house.

"Yeah, I know. We'll talk later."

Paula didn't want to go home, so she went to her brother's house. She showed him the gun and explained everything that had happened.

"You need to lay low for a while," Mitch advised, "in case he goes to the police. He probably won't, though, since he's dealing." Her brother gently removed the gun from Paula's shaking hands. He gave his younger sister a hug.

"Okay, I will. I was so angry when he slapped me, I just lost it."

"I know, but you could have killed him or someone else. I gave you that gun because of the break-ins in your neighborhood. Not for you to go nuts and shoot a nigga in the foot. Go stay with Lottie for a few days. I'll see what the rumors are about this and I'll get back to you."

For the next week, Paula spent more time at her sister's than at her own home. She was aware that a lot of people had seen her shoot Frankie. *I can't go to jail for this. I need to leave town and get away from here for a while. I have the baby now, and I have to be here to take care of her. How could I be so stupid? It just wasn't worth the risk of being away from my baby.*

Paula continuously berated herself. Over the next several days she decided that she had to leave Marion, if just for a little while. She was jittery all the time, always afraid she would run into Frankie B. and he'd try to hurt her. She asked Mitch to give her car an oil change and tune-up. She'd be leaving for Minneapolis as soon as possible. Mitch insisted on coming with her; they left the next weekend. She made arrangements to stay with her cousin Charlotte and her family until she could find an apartment for her and her little girl.

Frankie B. never went to the police, but Paula felt better living in Minneapolis. She stayed in contact with Shannon, and they planned for Shannon to come during the next summer shut-down at RCA, which was a month away.

Meanwhile, Shannon couldn't stop thinking about the shooting and how she wanted something better for her and the kids. She was afraid Frankie would come after her for what Paula had done. She decided she too needed a break from being in Marion. She would take her kids to Minneapolis for a two-week vacation.

On the last day before the annual shutdown, as soon as she got home from work, Shannon packed up the kids and hit the road for Minneapolis. Only she didn't know she would never return to Marion again.

CHAPTER 13

Shannon and her kids arrived at her sister's house in Minneapolis on a Saturday in June 1977. It was midmorning and she was tired, but she talked to her sister and her nieces for a while before lying down for a nap. When she woke, she called Paula to let her know she had arrived.

"What are you doing now?" asked Paula. "I may swing by after I run to the store."

"I'll be around here. I'm hoping some of my brothers and sisters come by so I can see everyone. If not, I'm sure I'll get to see everyone eventually before I head back to Marion."

"Okay, then, I'll see you in about an hour," Paula said.

Paula arrived at Charlotte and Eddie's house soon after. They were so happy to see each other; they hugged and talked as though they hadn't seen each other in years, while their children played on the floor nearby. Other family members came by for quick visits.

That night, after the other visitors had left, Charlotte volunteered to watch the children while Paula and Shannon went for a drive. They drove around Lake Nokomis in South Minneapolis a few times while they talked, laughed, and reminisced. They talked about what each of them wanted for their future. After they left the lake, they drove through downtown, admiring all the skyscrapers and the breathtaking skyline. It was one of the most beautiful sights they had ever seen. All the lights were shining brightly on the warm summer night. The stars sparkled in the sky as they drove around the mansions surrounding Lake Calhoun.

"It's so nice here. I really don't want to go back to Marion," said Shannon.

"I know, I really like it here," Paula replied. "There's so much to do—and I already have a decent job."

"Yeah, if I could get a good job, I would move here too." Shannon was dreaming of a positive life for her and for her children, Lamont and Teresa.

"I gotta get home so I can get up for work tomorrow. Let's plan on going out sometime next weekend. There's several nightclubs we can go to."

"Okay, let's see if anyone else wants to go too. It'll be fun," said Shannon.

Back at Charlotte's, they talked while Paula got her daughter ready to go home. "I'll talk to you later on this week and we'll definitely go out," said Paula as she left.

That week, Shannon and her kids went shopping, saw movies, and visited family members. One of Shannon's sisters offered to babysit the kids now and then so Shannon could have some adult time. They all enjoyed their days and evenings with family and friends, relaxing in the warmth of the summer at the lakes and at parties.

The following Saturday, the family held a cookout at a local park. That evening, several of the grown-ups went out to a nightclub. They danced, drank, and laughed the night away. Some of their group eventually left, but Shannon, Paula, and a few friends stayed.

"Girl, aren't you glad you came?" Paula asked when they returned to their table after dancing to a couple of songs.

"Whew!" Shannon said, sitting down and dabbing at her face with a napkin. "Yeah, thank you for talking me into getting out for a little bit."

"You needed to get out and relax after all that mess in Marion."

"I just didn't want to leave the kids at home after only being here for a few days," said Shannon.

A light-skinned black man with light-brown eyes approached their table. "Would you like to dance?" he asked Shannon.

"Sure." She took a sip of her drink and stood up. They danced to a couple of songs, talking and laughing the entire time. When the next song started playing, Shannon told him she was going back to the table.

"Thanks for the dance," the man said. He watched Shannon return to her table.

"I've had so much fun tonight!" Shannon said, sitting at the table with Paula. "And that man I was dancing with seems so nice."

"Which one? I know you ain't talking about that old-ass man!" Paula laughed. "I noticed him staring at you a lot, especially when you were dancing with other men. It was kind of creepy."

"He ain't that old. He seemed harmless enough. Besides, he ain't like the losers I've been seeing. He sounds educated, smooth." Shannon laughed.

"Girl, you're crazy. So what's his name? He looks familiar to me," said Paula. "Like one of the older dudes from Marion or somewhere. I know I've seen him before."

"His name is weird; I can't remember how to pronounce it. It starts with a Z or a J or something."

"Did he ask for your number? I know Charlotte and Eddie won't like you having all these men calling their phone."

"What do you mean 'all these men'? And I didn't give their number out. I got *his* number," said Shannon proudly.

"That's good, because you don't want to piss them off—then they won't want you to stay with them anymore."

"Don't I know it," agreed Shannon.

They stayed at the club until it closed. As they were leaving, the man approached them and asked if they needed a ride.

"No thanks, we drove," said Paula, annoyed. She hated it when people assumed she needed something from them.

"Okay. I just want to make sure you beautiful ladies get home safely," the man said.

"I bet," Paula mumbled. "So what's your name, anyway?"

"Xavier. And you are?"

"I'm Paula, Shannon's cousin."

"Nice to meet you. Can I escort you to your car?" Xavier asked.

"Sure," said Shannon as Paula rolled her eyes. "We're parked just around the corner." They had a friendly conversation as they walked to Paula's car, taking their time to enjoy the full moon and warm air.

"Well, here we are. Thank you for walking with us," said Shannon.

"You're welcome; now make sure you call me. I'd like to take you out to dinner sometime."

"I'll call you soon," promised Shannon as Paula got into the driver's seat and started the engine. "Bye."

"Goodnight, ladies," Xavier said as he shut the door for Shannon.

Paula and Shannon drove in silence for a few moments. "So what did you think of him?" Shannon asked.

"Honestly, there is something about him that seems familiar. I heard of a Xavier before; is he from Marion?"

"I don't know. I didn't ask him where he's from or anything. We were just having a good time and all. We'll talk more when we go out to dinner."

"*If* you go out to dinner, you mean. Just be careful with him—I get a bad feeling about him, but I don't know why," Paula warned her cousin.

"Girl, I will. You worry too much."

"Get to know him before you let yourself get all gaga over this man. And remember, he is a lot older and has a lot more experience than you."

"Why are you saying this shit to me?" Shannon asked.

"Because of your track record with choosing raunchy men to be with. I don't want you to be hurt. I love you and care about you," Paula said.

"Don't go getting all crazy on me—I'm only gonna be here for two weeks anyway. So did you meet anyone interesting?" Shannon tried to divert the conversation away from her.

"As a matter of fact, I did. We'll see how things go, but I'm really not trying to get serious with anyone. I just want to have fun sometimes, between working and raising Shondra."

"Yeah, I know what you mean. We gotta take care of our kids, but we can still can have fun, too."

"So when are you going to call Xavier?" Paula asked. "I swear he looks really familiar."

"I was going to call him when we get back to Charlotte's house."

"Girl, don't do that. You'll seem too eager. Wait a couple of days and make him think you aren't that interested in him," Paula urged her cousin.

"I'm only gonna be here less than two weeks longer, remember?" Shannon said in a sarcastic tone.

"Okay, okay. You don't have to get mad at me. I'm just telling you what I would do."

"I'm sorry, but every time I meet someone, all of y'all act like I ain't got any sense. I am here on vacation and I want to have a good time. If some old dude wants to take me out and spend some money on me, I'm game," Shannon said, laughing.

"You know when they start spending money on you they expect sex in return, and they think they own you!" Paula couldn't believe her cousin was so flip about serious things. She worried about her sometimes.

On their way back to Charlotte's, they stopped at the White Castle on Lake Street. It was the place to go after the clubs closed. They had greasy, cheap little square burgers and fish sandwiches, with light-brown crinkle fries; it all tasted real good after partying most of the night.

They made it back to Shannon's sister's house just after two in the morning. "Let me know how it goes when you call Xavier, and where you decide to go for dinner," Paula said.

"I will, and you let me know if you get with the mystery man. Maybe we can go on a double date," Shannon replied.

"We'll see," Paula said. "I'll be talking with ya."

"Okay, see ya soon."

Shannon called Xavier the next day. She'd intended to wait a couple of days, but that night she dreamed about his bright smile and pleasant voice. She couldn't stop thinking about him.

They planned to meet at a little café for lunch, not far from Charlotte's. Shannon got there first, so she was seated and ordered a soft drink.

Xavier arrived and spotted her at a table next to a window. "Hello, Miss Lady," Xavier said. He kissed her on the cheek.

Oh, wow, he's a smooth one. "Hello, Xavier." Shannon smiled up at him.

"Have you been here long?" he asked.

"Not long. About ten minutes," Shannon replied. "I didn't order yet."

"Well, let's see if we can get a waitress over here." Xavier beckoned a waitress and they ordered their food.

"So what else do you like to do in your spare time besides pick up men in nightclubs?" Xavier asked.

"What? I don't ..." They both laughed as Shannon realized he was joking. "Oh, you're very funny. But to answer your question, I love roller-skating, watching movies, dancing, and shopping. But most of all I love doing things with my family, especially my kids."

"Well, how many kids do you have?"

"Two. A girl and a boy. Do you have any kids?"

"No, I don't have any," Xavier lied.

Uh, he's got to be in his late thirties, and no kids. That's a bit strange. "Oh. What do you do for work?"

"I'm in banking and finance."

"That sounds interesting. What bank do you work at?" Shannon asked.

"Twin City Federal. Yeah, it's a local bank." *Damn, I gotta stop answering her about me. Where is that waitress with our food?*

They continued making small talk while they ate. When they finished and the waitress brought the check, Shannon reached for it to pay her part.

"No, let me. It's my treat," Xavier said.

"I can pay for my own lunch," Shannon said.

"No, I want to pay. Let's just say I am a bit old-fashioned."

"Okay." *Not bad, an old-fashioned type of man. That's a nice difference from the younger boys I usually deal with.*

After paying for their lunch, Xavier walked Shannon to her car. "Can I call you later on tonight?" Xavier asked.

"I'll call you. I'm not sure what I'll be doing later, but I'll try to call."

"That'll be good." Xavier smiled at her and took her hand, raising it to his lips. "Bye for now, Miss Lady."

Oh, he is so charming! "Good-bye, Xavier."

Later that evening, Shannon told Charlotte and their sisters Deana and Roslyn about Xavier.

"He sounds real smart when he talks, and he's so good-looking. He likes having fun like I do," Shannon explained as a big smile spread across her face.

"What's his name?"

"What does he look like?"

"What kind of job does he have?"

Shannon's sisters bombarded her with questions. "Whoa! One question at a time. First, his name is Xavier. He's medium height and muscular. He has caramel-colored skin and a bright smile with deep dimples."

"Wait, you said his name is Xavier?" asked Roslyn, sipping her beer. "Where is he from? Is he from Marion?"

"Yes, his name is Xavier. No, I assume he's from here. Why?" Shannon asked. "Do you know him?"

"I don't know, but he sounds a lot like the Xavier who Monica used to mess with back in Marion. You know her son is supposed to be his."

"He can't be the same person. There's no way," Shannon tried to convince her sisters.

"Yeah, you're probably right," Roslyn agreed—but she couldn't get the thought out of her head that they were indeed the same man. She had heard that Xavier from Marion had left in a hurry because he was wanted for robberies in and around Marion and a bank robbery in Indianapolis.

"If he is the same person, you need to stay away from him," Roslyn warned. "He is a nasty, evil person."

"She's got that right. I hope for your sake it ain't the same guy," Charlotte said.

"I don't think he's the same guy. Besides, he said he doesn't have any kids."

"Men don't always claim their kids. Especially someone like the Xavier I'm thinking of," said Roslyn.

"Well, just wait until you all meet him. We're going to Lake Calhoun tomorrow. When he picks me up, you can meet him and you'll see. He can't be the same person," Shannon insisted.

"We can't tomorrow—I promised to take the girls shopping in the morning and then I'll be in the salon the rest of the day and evening." Charlotte said.

"We're having a cookout next weekend," Deana offered. "Why don't you invite him?"

"Okay, that's a plan," Shannon said.

The following day, Shannon went to the beach with Xavier. When he knocked on the door, Shannon ran to answer it, dressed in bright-yellow shorts and a matching halter top. It fit perfectly on her petite frame. She opened the door with a big smile.

"Hi, come on in," she greeted him.

"Hello. Damn, you look good!" Xavier couldn't take his eyes off her sexy, dark-brown skin against the yellow clothes. He glanced at her stunning long legs flowing from the bottom of her shorts. *Mmm, mmm, mmm,* he thought, pulling his gaze back to her face.

"So do you," she replied, still smiling. "I'll just be a second; I need to let them know I'm leaving." She ran upstairs.

Xavier remained by the door, looking at the décor of the living room. He saw pictures of Charlotte's children, and then he saw the picture of Charlotte and her husband. Xavier's smile faded. *Well, I'll be damned. Her sister is married to Lee Ann's cousin Eddie. This is going to be interesting! I've got to stay away from her family for now.*

"Okay, I'm ready," Shannon said as she returned to the living room. She noticed Xavier looking at the picture of Charlotte and Eddie. "That's my sister Charlotte and her husband Eddie."

"Oh, okay. Let's go, the lake is waiting for us." He smiled.

It was a hot, sunny day—perfect for the lake. On the way, they talked and listened to the radio. Shannon sat close to Xavier and held his hand while he drove. When they arrived, she and Xavier walked around the lake a couple of times, talking and holding hands. Every so often they would stop and kiss and just gaze out at the water. Then they sat at a picnic bench, watching people walking their dogs, playing with children, and having a good time listening to music from their cars and boom boxes. Shannon felt close to him; she really liked him.

"Are you hungry?" Xavier asked, taking her hand. "Let's go get something to eat."

"Yeah. Where should we go?" They walked back to his car.

"How about Jack's Shack? The ribs are out of this world. After we eat I have some things I need to take care of."

"Oh, okay," Shannon replied, disappointed. She wanted to spend more time with Xavier.

"Why are you sounding so down?" he asked with a chuckle. "I'll make it up to you tomorrow night. How about I take you out to dinner at a real classy place downtown?"

"Ooh! That sounds nice. I guess that will make up for you cutting out early on me."

"So I'll pick you up at six o'clock. How does that sound?"

"I have to see if someone will be able to watch my kids," Shannon replied.

"Okay. Let me know when I call you later tonight."

"Yeah, I will," she said, smiling up at him.

"All right, now that's better—to see that smile on your face again." He smiled too, taking her in his arms and kissing her so deeply it took her breath away.

They were kissing so passionately that people began to stare. Shannon opened her eyes and pulled away, breaking the kiss. "That was, um, nice," she said, trying to catch her breath.

"Yeah, I like how your soft, delicious lips feel on my mouth. See how good we are together?" Xavier chuckled.

"I do see." Shannon planted her mouth on his for a second kiss. This time they were tonguing each other. When they came up for air, they were both dizzy with delight. *Damn, he's a great kisser. If he's kissing that good, I wonder what he can do to me in bed.* Shannon gazed into his sparkling light-brown eyes.

As he pulled back from the kiss, Xavier said, "Maybe we better go get that lunch before we get too carried away out here, in front of all these people." He didn't want to stop, but he knew he had to get going. *Damn, I could have her back to my place and in bed within the hour. But I'm supposed to meet Jessica at three. I'll see how lunch goes.* They walked arm-in-arm back to Xavier's car.

After lunch, when they got back into the car, Xavier handed Shannon $300 and said, "Here, take this to buy yourself something nice to wear when we go out to dinner tomorrow night."

She was taken aback. "I can't take this from you."

"Why can't you? It's just a little gift for a beautiful lady. I want to do nice things for you, make you happy and make sure you have the things you desire."

"How dare you! You think I'm a whore or something? You have to pay for my time and a little making out?"

"No, I just want to keep seeing that pretty smile on your face!"

"Well, you can put that money back in your damn wallet. You can't buy me or my happiness. I'm not for sale."

"All right, fine. I'll keep my money. I promise you I wasn't trying to treat you like a whore—I just wanted you to have a nice dress for tomorrow. It's a pretty fancy restaurant we're going to. That's all."

"Well, I can buy my own damn dress!"

"I didn't mean to offend you."

"Don't ever do that shit again."

"So if we start going steady, does that mean I can't buy you things or give you money?"

"That would be different. This is—what, our second date? It's very offensive."

"All right, it won't happen again. Are we okay now?"

"Yeah. But you do remember I have to go back home soon, right? I'm only here for a couple weeks, and then back to work."

Xavier's hazel eyes sparkled in the sunlight. "I know you're going back home, but there's nothing wrong with us enjoying each other and having fun while you're here, is there?"

Shannon gazed into his eyes and smiled. "No, I suppose not."

Xavier dropped her off back at Charlotte's house, deciding to keep his meeting. As they walked to the door, he promised to call her later. They kissed some more before Shannon went inside. Charlotte was still working in the shop and Eddie wasn't home from the steel factory yet, so Shannon didn't invite him in; she knew he had to run some errands. They said their good-byes, Shannon still wishing he didn't have to leave.

She went into the house smiling hard. She was so taken by Xavier; she stood at the door for a few moments with her arms across her chest, reminiscing about their day and anticipating their date tomorrow night.

Charlotte's oldest daughter, Winnie, was sitting on the couch watching television. Shannon hadn't even noticed her. "Aunt Shannon, are you okay? Why are you standing there smiling?"

"Uh … oh, I was just thinking of how much fun I had today, that's all. What are you watching?" she asked, trying to pull herself together. She couldn't get Xavier out of her head; she could think of nothing but him. She shivered when she thought about the kisses they had shared. She didn't even hear Winnie's reply.

The next day, Shannon and Paula went to Southdale Center, a mall in Edina, a nearby suburb of Minneapolis. She found a pretty red-and-black dress and some nice black heels. The dress fit her as if it was made especially for her, accenting her small waist and round butt.

"You look beautiful," Paula told her when she came out of the dressing room.

"Thank you. Do you think it's okay for the Orion Room?"

"I've never been there, but I'm sure it'll be perfect."

"Okay. I want to look good tonight. I am so anxious to see him again. He does something to me—I don't even know how to explain it."

"Whoa, you don't even really know him," said Paula.

"I know, but anyway, I could see myself with him. We're good together—I can just tell."

"What time is he picking you up?"

"At seven. I can hardly wait! Let me pay for this; I need to get home to get ready."

Paula went out into the mall while Shannon paid for the clothes. When she came out of the store, she saw Paula talking to a woman who looked familiar; Shannon wasn't sure where she'd seen her before.

"Hey, girl, I'm all ready now," Shannon said as she approached Paula and the other woman.

"Oh, there you are. Shannon, this is Eddie's cousin, Lee Ann," Paula said.

"Hi, Lee Ann. I'm Charlotte's sister."

"Hi," Lee Ann replied. "Well, I have to get going."

"Okay, bye."

Shannon was so excited; she thought only of Xavier the whole way home, smiling to herself but saying little to her cousin. Back at Charlotte's, she quickly ran upstairs to the room she was sharing with her children. She took a shower and then polished her nails a shade of red she'd borrowed from Charlotte to match her dress. When her nails had dried, she did her hair and applied a small amount of makeup. She put on her new dress and shoes.

Fifteen minutes later, the doorbell rang. She asked Xavier to come in while she said goodnight to her children. As Shannon and Xavier walked to his car, Charlotte and Eddie were getting out of their car.

"Hi, Charlotte and Eddie! This is my friend Xavier."

"Nice to meet you, Xav—" Charlotte started to say. As she turned around, she stopped midsentence. Damn, it was the same Xavier from Marion!

CHAPTER 14

Eddie just stared at Xavier. He knew this cat was married to his cousin, Lee Ann Baldwin.

"What's happening, Eddie and Charlotte," Xavier said.

"What's up with you?" asked Eddie.

"I'm taking Shannon out to dinner."

From the look on her sister's face, Shannon knew this was the same man from Marion her sisters had been talking about.

"So you all know each other?" Shannon asked.

"Yeah, we know each other," said Charlotte. "He's married to Eddie's cousin Lee Ann. I don't think you should get involved with him."

"What? You're married? To Lee Ann?" Shannon asked Xavier.

"No. Well, legally, yes. Come on, Charlotte. You know me and Lee Ann haven't been living together for damn near five years."

"Stop, all of you—just stop it. I'm going out to dinner with him and we can talk when I get home."

"No, you're not going anywhere with him!" Charlotte said, grabbing Shannon's arm. "We need to talk *now*, and you need to listen to what I'm saying!"

Shannon glared at her sister and tried to yank her arm away. "Yes, I am. I'll talk to you later. Let go of me, damn it!" Pulling her arm free from Charlotte's grasp, she stormed off toward Xavier's car.

"Okay, okay. We will surely be talking when you get back—and you best believe I have a lot to say!" Charlotte shouted.

Charlotte was really pissed off. She and Eddie walked into the house and Shannon and Xavier got into his car and drove away. "I can't believe she won't listen to me," Charlotte fumed. "And he had to have known we're sisters, because he picked her up here yesterday when they went to the lake. He had to know."

"Maybe he didn't. He hasn't been here with Lee Ann. Remember, we moved a little bit after they stopped living together," Eddie reminded Charlotte.

"But I just don't trust him about anything. He's such a manipulator and a liar. All he wants is to hurt people. He's been in prison since he's been in Minneapolis—and who knows what he was really up to in Marion. Oh, and let's not forget how he uses and beats on women. He damn near mutilated Lee Ann. I will not let my sister get involved with that monster," Charlotte's voice was filled with disgust and anger.

"I know," Eddie said, "but she's a grown-up, and you can't make her not be with the man. All we can do is talk to her and hope she listens. We can try to protect her and encourage her to go to the police when it gets bad. Other than that, there ain't a damn thing for us to do. You know I love my cousin, and we all tried to tell her to go back to Marion and leave that fool alone. She went back, but soon as she was old enough to leave home she came running right back to him. I would like to put a bullet in his head, though."

"I know you're right, Shannon is an adult—but I still can't help how I feel about the whole mess. I hoped for Shannon that he wasn't the same Xavier. I am gonna stay up until she comes back, because we need to have a very serious talk with her."

"Good. But don't be surprised if she doesn't listen to you."

"I won't be, but I won't feel right if I don't at least try to talk with her."

Charlotte and her family ate dinner, and then she called a couple of her sisters to tell them what she'd discovered about Shannon's new friend. They were all disappointed, and they each knew there would be nothing they could do to discourage their sister from getting involved with him once she'd made up her mind. Charlotte and Eddie watched a couple of movies while they waited for Shannon to return home. Charlotte was able to laugh during a comedy they watched, but her mind continuously wandered back to Shannon. Every time she thought of her sister with that man, she felt sick to her stomach.

She tried to stay awake until Shannon got home, but she fell asleep on the couch while waiting. When she woke up and headed to bed, she saw that it was after five in the morning. *Damn it!* she thought as she fell asleep.

The next morning, Charlotte showered, dressed and went downstairs to join Eddie for breakfast before her first appointment arrived. She was hoping to speak with Shannon before she had to get into the shop, but it seemed Shannon was not up yet.

Charlotte made herself some coffee, eggs, and toast. As she sat on the living-room sofa to eat, she heard Shannon come down the stairs and go into the kitchen. She was already dressed and looked ready to go out for the day. Her kids were with her.

"You're up early," Charlotte said. "Can we talk for a few minutes?"

"Sure, let me give the kids some cereal. Come on, Teresa and Lamont, sit down and eat your cereal before we leave." Shannon grabbed a cup of coffee and they went into the living room. Eddie sat next to his wife on the sofa; Shannon sat on the loveseat.

"So what do you want to talk about?" Shannon asked Charlotte, although she already knew the answer.

She'd had so much fun with Xavier last night. He treated her like a queen—opening doors for her, pulling out her chair at dinner, making her feel special. They had gone to a posh hotel afterward, but she wouldn't tell Charlotte that. They had just talked and gotten to know each other better; they'd both fallen asleep watching television.

"I need you to just listen to everything I'm about to tell you about Xavier," demanded Charlotte.

"Okay, go on and tell me what you have to say." Shannon couldn't hide her defensive attitude.

"You already know he has a baby with Monica," Charlotte said.

"Yeah, so what? I'm just going out with him while I'm here. It's not like I plan on having a life with him."

"I know that, but he was real mean to her and he beat her up a couple of times. He also robs places. He robbed all kinds of stores and banks in Indiana and he's doing the same thing here. Do you really want to be with someone like that, someone who's been in and out of jail? What if he does something while you and the kids are out? Do you really want your kids around his lifestyle?"

"He's not going to be around my kids," Shannon insisted.

"It doesn't matter. He's crazy! He's a manipulator and all he cares about is money. He doesn't care about people or what he does to them. It's all a game to him. He will manipulate you into doing whatever he wants you to do—and then he will hurt you as soon as you do something he doesn't like or you don't do what he wants. He is very dangerous!" Charlotte couldn't contain her emotions. She was aware that she knew only a part of what he was capable of.

"He sure doesn't seem dangerous to me," Shannon replied. "He was a perfect gentleman last night and he didn't even try to have sex with me or anything. He doesn't seem to have a mean streak like you're saying."

"That's how he is at first: all kind, saying and doing all the right things. Then, when you're head over heels, he starts treating you like shit!"

"Maybe he's different from when you knew him. People do change."

"You haven't known him that long, though. Have you heard what he did to Lee Ann? Not just the beating, but the worse thing he did to her?"

"No. What was he supposed to have done to her?"

"During one of his stints in jail, Lee Ann started hanging out with some guy who lived in her apartment building. Xavier had people watching her, so he knew everything she was doing. He called her and questioned her about it. After he got out he went to her apartment and just went crazy on her. He beat her so badly she had bruises everywhere on her body. He gave her a black eye and busted her lip."

"That's terrible. Really awful," Shannon said.

Eddie chimed in. "My cousin said Xavier beat her with a broom in addition to his fists. Not only did he beat her with it, but he rammed it inside of her, over and over again—so many times she almost died from all the damage it did to her insides. He raped her with a broom, damn it!" Now Eddie was yelling. "And the whole time, he kept telling her she was his and if she ever cheated on him again he would kill her. She was hurt so bad she couldn't walk or anything for damn near three months. The sick son of a bitch! If you think he won't hurt you too, then you are just as crazy as he is!" Eddie got up and stormed out of the house.

He had to cool off. He was still angry with his cousin because she took Xavier back, over and over, even after all of that. *I just don't understand what is with these young girls. The nigga throws some money their way and they act like they ain't got no sense whatsoever. I can't help them. I tried talking to Lee Ann and she wouldn't listen, and now Shannon. Why are they so damn crazy about this dude? Well, at least Shannon will be leaving in a few days and she won't be around him.* Eddie walked around the block. He was so frustrated he didn't know what to do.

Back at the house, Charlotte and Shannon continued talking. "I was just trying to have some fun for the few weeks I was here. I would've stayed in Marion if I'd known my going out on a couple dates was going to cause all this mess."

"You going out on a few dates isn't the problem. The problem is the person you met and dated is a real bad dude. We don't want anything bad to happen to you."

"Okay, I will keep that in mind. I won't be seeing him again before I leave, anyway."

A few days passed. Shannon hung out with her cousins and didn't go out with Xavier, as she had said she wouldn't.

The evening before Shannon and her kids were supposed to leave, Shannon asked Charlotte and Eddie, "Can I talk to you?"

"Sure," said Charlotte.

"I've decided not to go back to Marion. I want to build a life here for me and my kids. There are more job opportunities here than in Marion, and better schools. I just want a fresh start."

"Are you staying because you really want a fresh start, or because you want to be with Xavier?" Charlotte asked.

"I'm not seeing him," she lied. "I've wanted to live here ever since you moved here and I would come to visit. I even told Paula I wanted to live here some day. I'm tired of being in Marion. I want something new and exciting for us."

"Well, living here is a big change from living in Marion. I do understand that you want more," said Charlotte. "It sounds like you've made up your mind, and you are grown woman—but you need to call Mom and Dad to let them know. And don't forget to tell RCA you won't be coming back."

"I have made up my mind. I'll move out as soon as I can find my own place—if that's okay with both of you?"

"We love having you and the children here," Eddie said, "but I am still worried about you seeing that Xavier dude. I don't want him around here at all. And yes, you can stay here as long as Charlotte is okay with it."

"I don't mind," Charlotte said. "But I don't want to hear that you've gotten back involved with that crazy man again."

"I won't. And thanks, both of you. I've already put in several job applications and I've been looking at places to rent close to here. I'll be out of here within a few weeks at the most!" Shannon gave each of them a hug and went upstairs.

"I sure hope this isn't a mistake," Charlotte said quietly to Eddie. "I think she's been true to her word about not seeing that fool any more. I just pray it stays that way."

CHAPTER 15

Two weeks later, Shannon found a three-bedroom duplex not far from Charlotte and Eddie's home and close to other family members as well. It was on the upper floor of a large old house that had been converted into two separate homes. She had saved some money from her job at RCA. One of her brothers packed up her small apartment in Marion and drove everything to Minneapolis for her.

She hadn't told anyone that she'd started seeing Xavier again. She had so much fun when she was with him; she just didn't see in him what Charlotte and Eddie were telling her. She didn't believe he was capable of the things her sisters and Eddie had described. She would decide for herself what type of person Xavier really was. She continued to do things with him. By now he was frequently giving her large sums of money, and she was accepting them. Xavier was kind to her kids, and they were fond of him. They went to movies, the lakes, summer festivals, and concerts.

Eventually, the two became sexually intimate—and that was all it took for Shannon. He was a great lover, got along with her kids, helped her out financially; they got along so well, she thought they had great karma. He seemed to be just what she was looking for— and a big change from the other dudes she had been with in Marion.

In Minneapolis Shannon found a job she enjoyed, as a sales clerk at an upscale department store. She would be able to cover her living expenses for a while and would still look for a job that paid more. With the money Xavier gave her, she bought plush furniture and real fur rugs. She had all of the latest fashions in clothes, shoes, purses, and jewelry. Teresa and Lamont had enough clothes and toys for five kids.

Shannon was happy with her new life. After she'd set up her new place just the way she wanted it, she invited her cousin Paula over. They were sitting around watching television, talking, and smoking reefer, catching up the way they always had.

"This is real nice," said Paula. "I love the way you've decorated and everything."

"Thank you!" said Shannon proudly, looking around at her new living room. "I had fun picking out all the furniture, drapes, rugs, and knickknacks. I wanted everything to match perfectly."

"How in the world did you get the place and all this furniture so fast? When I talked to you a couple weeks ago, you were just beginning to look for a place. What a miracle!" Paula said sarcastically. She suspected Xavier had paid for everything, including the groceries.

"Don't tell anyone, but I started seeing Xavier again. He gave me some money to get all set up, and he keeps giving me money. He's really glad I stayed."

"Do you know how he's making all that money?" Paula asked.

"He said he owns a couple of businesses and works in banking."

"Girl, that's not what I heard. I heard he's been in and out of prison for having guns on him, and he's suspected for robbing places. He don't own shit," said Paula, chuckling. "And yeah, he's into banks, all right—robbing them!"

"He's telling me he makes his money in a legal profession, and I haven't seen any of the crap you all keep talking about. So until I see different, I'm gonna believe him and keep on seeing him. You know good and well you'd let him give you money if he was interested in you, wouldn't you?"

"Not really. Especially not when my family is telling me the dude is heavy into some illegal stuff—he's a manipulator and beats women. Now, if a man is really working a real job and wants to help me out, I'm all for that. But don't let yourself get hooked on his money and then get caught up in his mess."

"I'm not. It's not about the money; I do go to work every day. Ain't nobody ever helped me like this. He's good to me and my kids. We have fun together," Shannon said.

"I understand all that, but I can't tell you enough about the bad vibes I get from that guy. I know I've only been around him a couple times, but after hearing what Charlotte and everyone else says about him, when I do see him I get the creeps!"

"I hear what you're saying, but I have to take that chance because you don't know him like I do. Now let's eat something, I got the munchies!" Shannon said.

They munched on chips while they fried the chicken wings Shannon had taken out to thaw earlier that day. They laughed and talked about old times and told each other what they had planned for the week. Shannon was going to be working all week and then do some more shopping. Paula was working and going to a friend's cookout on the weekend. They talked while they ate and cleaned up the kitchen.

They had just sat down in the living room to watch TV when they heard a knock on the door. Paula lit a cigarette while Shannon got up to answer the door. It was Xavier.

"Hey, baby," said Xavier as he hugged and kissed Shannon. She could taste liquor on his breath.

"Hey yourself! You remember my cousin Paula," said Shannon, hugging Xavier back.

"Oh, what's up Paula?" Xavier greeted her.

"Hi. I came by to see Shannon's new place. She really did a nice job decorating it, don't you think?" Paula tried to hide the disgust she felt toward him.

"Yeah, did real good—with my money." Xavier was slurring his words slightly. Shannon was stunned by his comment.

"Why'd you say it like that?" Paula asked. "You *gave* her the money, didn't you?"

"Yeah, I gave it to her. She wouldn't be here if it weren't for me helping her."

"That's not true," Paula argued. "She was determined to stay here with or without help from you. So you're the type of brother that does things for people but wants everyone to know about it? That's silly. I can't stand people like that."

"Bitch, who do you think you are? You think you just gonna come in here and insult me after I'm the only one helping your cousin out? I don't believe this shit!" Xavier yelled.

"Why are you acting like this?" asked Shannon. "You insisted I take the money, and you didn't say or act like it was a big deal. So what's the problem now?"

"There is no problem. I was just saying, you wouldn't have all of this if it weren't for me."

"I can make it on my own. I would never have accepted it from you in the first place if I'd known that you just wanted to be noticed for it. I can't stand niggas like you, acting like they want to help you out of the kindness of their hearts, only to throw it in your face later on. Well, don't do me any favors. I will pay you back every dime, and you can stay the hell away from me!" Shannon yelled. Paula looked at the two of them, shaking her head.

"Baby, don't be like that. I guess I just had too much to drink. I didn't mean what I said."

"Yes you did," Paula jumped in. "I've seen too many so-called men like you to know you meant *exactly* what you said."

"Ain't nobody talking to you, girl!" Xavier yelled at Paula, stepping closer to her as if he would hit her.

"That's enough of this shit, Xavier," Shannon said. "You better not ever act like you're gonna touch my cousin again. Why don't you just leave? You've been drinking and you can't come in here acting stupid and shit."

"You jus' gonna make me leave? Well, damn, you are really sumfthing," Xavier said as he stumbled to the door.

"Just leave," Shannon said again. She opened the door and he left.

Soon after, Paula gathered her belongings. "Girl, I need to get home. Are you sure you'll be okay?"

"Yeah, I'll be fine. He's gone, anyway. I'll call you tomorrow."

Shannon was dozing off in front of the TV when someone began knocking on her door. She looked through the peephole and saw Xavier. She let him in and confronted him about his behavior, especially acting like he was going to hit Paula. "So the things people are saying about you are true. You disrespect people—especially women. You're a manipulator and you probably lied to me about how you really make your money!"

"What are you talking about? I don't disrespect women or manipulate them. And how I make my money ain't nobody's business. All you need to do is be thankful I help you out."

"If you don't mind so much, why did you throw it in my face that you helped me? I'd rather struggle than have any man do that to me. And you just keep bringing it up—why is that?"

"I already told you I had too much to drink, that's all," Xavier said. "I said I was sorry, but you keep going back to it."

"*I* keep going back to it? You just got done saying I need to be thankful you helped me. That's some crazy bullshit, if you ask me. Don't try to twist it back on me," Shannon said, pointing a finger in his face.

"Bitch, if you don't get your finger out my damn face I will beat your ass," said Xavier. He grabbed her by the neck.

"Let go of me! You're crazy!" Shannon shouted, and he let go of her neck.

"Damn, I'm sorry, baby. Maybe I better leave for now."

"Yes, you need to leave right now," said Shannon in disbelief. Xavier was already walking out the front door.

Shannon sat on her couch wondering what had just happened. She had never seen this side of him. *I can't believe this. I guess my family may be right about him after all. I know he'd been drinking, but he didn't seem drunk enough to make him act that way. Besides, we've had drinks together before and he never acted like that. But sometimes people act totally different when they drink certain liquors. I don't know what to think. I'll see how he acts next time we're together.*

She got up to go to bed after locking her front door and checking on her kids. As she lay in bed, her mind drifted back to all of the fun times she'd had with Xavier up until tonight. She decided she would stick it out with him and see how things went from there.

Over the next few weeks, Shannon saw or spoke with Xavier almost every day. He showered her with the same kindness he had offered all along. She again convinced herself he was the man she believed him to be.

One night, after making love to Xavier, Shannon decided she wanted to know what he really did for a living. She was irritated that he didn't have a work number where she could reach him; she always had to wait for him to call her. She was tired of that; what if an emergency happened and she needed to contact him?

"That was wonderful baby," said Xavier, rolling off of her.

"I enjoyed it too," Shannon said, trying to catch her breath. She lay with her head on his chest trying to think of the best way to ask him about his job.

He was watching her face. "What are you thinking about?" he asked. "You look like you're deep in thought about something."

"I want to ask you something, but I don't know if I should or not."

"You know you can ask me anything. If I don't like the question I won't answer it." He kissed her neck and caressed her shoulder.

"I just don't want you to get mad, is all."

"I don't get mad over questions—they're just words. So ask me."

"Well, I just want to know what you really do to make the kind of money that you do. I mean, it doesn't matter—I will still love you and care about you. I just want to know the truth," she said softly.

Xavier was quiet for several minutes, gazing at the ceiling, his turn to be deep in thought. "Before I answer your question, let me tell you my upbringing." He told her of his life and how he eventually turned to crime.

"I'm sorry you went through all of that," Shannon said. "My family was on the poor side too, so I know how you must have felt, wanting to always have money."

"Does it bother you to know what I do?" asked Xavier.

"Yes—but I've dealt with drug dealers, shoplifters, and other shady people in my lifetime. I already thought there was something odd about your 'business.' Just don't ever ask me to take part in your jobs, and never, ever do any of it around my kids. I don't want them to ever know about what you do. They love you and I don't want them to think you're a bad person."

"I promise I will never involve them or you in any of my jobs. I wanted to tell you all about it, but I didn't want to lose you," Xavier said earnestly.

"I love you, Xavier. You don't have to be afraid to tell me anything."

"I won't be. And I love you, too." Xavier's gaze returned to the ceiling and his mind went into deep thoughts as he caressed Shannon's shoulder. She drifted into a deep sleep. *I don't know why I said that to her. I don't love anyone. I loved my family and they all turned away from me. I thought I loved Monica, but she ran from me and got me arrested for making me hit her in front of that damn cop back in Marion. The bitch took my son away from me. Then there's Lee Ann; now, she will do anything for me. She has always been infatuated with me. She's so weak and inferior. They all are. My mom, my sisters, Monica, Lee Ann, Jamie, Ira—all the whores of my life are so beneath me and they don't even know how I really feel about them all. They all think I loved them when I can't stand any of them. And now Shannon.*

Xavier eased out of the bed and went to the living room to call one of his girlfriends, who was going to help him rob a gun store.

"Hi, Jamie, it's me. Are you still up for tomorrow night?" he asked.

"Yeah, sure—I'm a little nervous but I'm ready. All I have to do is drive and be your lookout, right, baby?" she said. "And if anyone comes I honk my horn two short beeps and drive to the gas station around the corner and wait for you there."

"That's right, my lady. Pick me up at the Kmart on Lake Street at midnight. From there we go to the place and take care of business. I'll be in and out in two minutes tops. You don't need to be nervous."

"Okay, I'll be there at midnight. Promise me it will be all right."

"It will be. Just stay calm and no matter what happens, keep a cool head," said Xavier, trying to soothe her worries away.

"Okay, okay," Jamie said. "Bye, love."

"See ya." *I sure hope she doesn't mess this whole thing up. Maybe I should have talked Shannon into driving me. She's so much more at ease—but she's not into this kind of stuff. Anyway, it's too late now.*

Xavier turned to go back to the bedroom when he saw Shannon standing beside the sofa.

"Who was that?" she asked.

"Just a friend of mine who's going to help me out on some business. When did you get up?"

"Just a couple seconds ago."

"I had to make sure of the time me and a partner are meeting," said Xavier. "Let's go back to bed."

"Okay. I'm so sleepy." Shannon walked back to the bedroom, still half-asleep.

They slept until late morning. Teresa and Lamont woke around ten; Shannon got up to give them some cereal and turned the television on so they could watch cartoons. She went back to bed for another hour, until Xavier got up, showered, and dressed in one of the spare outfits he kept at her place. He went into the living room with the kids while Shannon showered and dressed.

"What are you watching?" he asked Teresa. "I haven't seen this one before."

"It's *Scooby-Doo!*" Teresa said. "You've never seen it?"

"Nope, I haven't. I don't watch cartoons," replied Xavier.

"That's silly—everybody watches cartoons!"

"Watch your mouth. Everyone doesn't watch cartoons." *Such a little smartass,* he thought. He shot Teresa a fake smile.

They watched the show until it ended and another cartoon started. A few minutes later, Shannon came out of the bathroom. She was fully dressed and beautiful.

"Hello, my babies, what should we do today?" she asked Lamont and Teresa.

"Park," said Lamont.

"I want to go to the movies," Teresa said.

"Let's go see a movie and then we can go to the park. And if you act right, we may get something to eat for dinner afterward." Shannon wanted to make both of her children happy.

"Thank you, Mommy!" Teresa cried.

"Thanks, Mommy!" Lamont squealed with excitement, clapping his hands.

"And what do you have planned for today?" asked Shannon as she turned to Xavier.

"I have a lot of business to take care of today and tonight. But I will call you first thing tomorrow morning and we can all go out for breakfast."

"That will be nice," Shannon said as she kissed him on his forehead.

"I guess I better get going."

"Bye, Xavier," said Teresa, and she gave him a hug good-bye.

"Bye, Teresa."

"Bye-bye," Lamont said in his cute two-year-old's voice.

"See you later, little guy."

After Xavier left, Shannon got the kids bathed and dressed. They went to the cinema and saw a children's movie while they ate popcorn and candy. Afterward, Shannon took them to play at a park near their house. She thought about all the stuff Xavier had shared with her about himself; she still wasn't sure he had been completely honest with her. She began to wonder if their relationship was something she really wanted.

On their way back they picked up some fast food and brought it home to eat. After dinner, Shannon gave the kids their baths, let them watch TV for an hour, and then put them to bed. As she got in her own bed to watch more TV, her thoughts returned to her relationship with Xavier. *Damn, I love him—and he does help me out sometimes. Do I want to give him up? I just can't yet.*

Summer turned to fall. Shannon enrolled Teresa in a nearby elementary school, and one of Shannon's sisters babysat Lamont while Shannon was at work. She and Xavier were as close as ever. He had never showed his violent side again, and she'd begun to do whatever he asked of her. She felt they had a great relationship. She didn't ask many questions about his work. He made her happy, and they usually had a lot of fun together—going to the movies, out to dinner, to a club, or to one of the lakes—or even just hanging out at her apartment.

One day during Labor Day weekend, Shannon, Xavier, and Paula were sitting around watching television and drinking. She and Paula had smoked some reefer. Xavier had drunk a few mixed drinks and a couple of beers throughout the evening. He began telling them about the different places he had robbed. He told them about the bank in Indianapolis and the small businesses in Marion and surrounding communities. He also told them about some of the places he'd hit there in Minneapolis.

"So I went in the store downtown right before it closed. I hid in the fitting room until they finally closed up the entire store. I went to the area where they kept all the money. I was able to open the safe after hours of trying. Then, when I had all the loot I could carry, I tried to leave but I couldn't get out. I had to stay in there all night until the doors unlocked the next morning."

"That's bullshit," said Paula. "There is no way you were in one of the largest department stores in downtown Minneapolis, and security didn't catch you. They keep that store highly guarded during the day and night."

"I swear it's true, I was stuck in there all night. So when the store opened the next morning, I left with the money and never went back. I had over fifty thousand dollars."

"I still don't believe you," said Paula.

"Baby, it does sound crazy," added Shannon.

"It was in the newspapers the next day and for a week after that. The store was robbed and they couldn't figure out how it happened. It was all me!" Xavier bragged. "I'm so good at what I do."

"So you meant to get locked in the store?" asked Shannon.

"Naw, Shannon, but I was quick at thinking and coming up with the idea of hiding out until a little after the store opened, then I walked around like I was a customer and I just walked out the front door. I'm brilliant."

"If you want to think so," said Paula, rolling her eyes.

"It's true," he insisted.

When they left Paula's house, Xavier told Shannon he didn't want her smoking weed with Paula anymore.

"Why the hell not?"

"Because I don't like her—and when you smoke weed with her, you get all smart-assed just the way she is. Besides, I said so."

Whenever they got together and Xavier had a few drinks, he wanted to brag about the robberies he had committed. One time, he and Shannon had gone out to dinner and had a couple of drinks. Afterward he took Shannon by Charlotte and Eddie's house to pick up Teresa and Lamont. Shannon went in the house while Xavier stayed in the car. Eddie had been sitting in the front yard talking with some of his cousins and brothers-in-law. Xavier got out of his car to smoke a cigarette. He said hi to the group of men and called Eddie over to the car.

"What's happening, Xavier?" Eddie asked as he approached the car.

"Not too much. I wanted to show you something." Xavier walked to the trunk of his car.

"What you got in there?" Eddie asked with suspicion.

"Get a look at that," Xavier replied as he unlocked the trunk and raised it just enough for Eddie to see its contents.

"What the hell? That's a lot of money you got back there." The entire space was filled with stacks of money, arranged by denomination: tens, twenties, fifties, and hundreds.

Xavier was proud of all the money he had. *Look at this dude's face. He wishes he had this type of dough!* "Keep your voice down, I don't want anyone to hear you," Xavier said, laughing as he shut the trunk and made sure it was locked. "You can have the same if you help me out with a few business dealings."

"Hell no! I know all about you and what you do. I won't be a part of any of it," Eddie said. As he walked back to the group of men, he could hear Xavier laughing.

"You're missing out on a good thing," Xavier yelled just as Shannon brought the kids out to the car.

"What was that about?" she asked after she'd situated the kids in the backseat.

"I just offered Eddie a business proposition."

Shannon didn't ask him anything about it. She knew her brother-in-law would never get involved with Xavier's "business" dealings.

Shannon noticed Xavier was out "on business" more often lately. She began to wonder if he was seeing another woman, because she saw less and less of him in the evenings. He was giving her more and more money, though, so she never complained.

In mid-October, Xavier had taken Shannon's car to the store, saying he was going out for a little while. He went to a local grocery store not far from her house and robbed the place. He had opened the safe and placed all the money in a duffel bag. As he was leaving, a security guard saw him and began to chase him through the parking lot.

"Stop or I'll shoot!" the guard yelled, but Xavier kept running. He tried to make it to the car. *Oh damn—I left the keys in the car with the engine still running!*

Another guard started running toward him from the direction of the car. Xavier was far enough away that he knew they'd likely miss him if they did shoot. He took a chance and began to zig-zag like he was on a football field, running out of the parking lot. Police cars began swarming the parking lot.

Xavier kept running until he found a place to hide, behind a house. He watched the guards as they gave up on chasing him because they'd lost sight of him. He could see the police officers in Shannon's car, looking for anything they could find on him.

Shit, that was too close, he thought as he rested to catch his breath. *How am I gonna get her car?*

CHAPTER 16

Xavier walked far away from the store, cutting through backyards and alleys whenever he saw that no one was around. He had gone about two miles west of the store and then cut back to Lake Street. He made his way back to Shannon's house and ran up the stairs. He banged on the door. "Come on, Shannon, it's me. Hurry up!" Xavier yelled.

"I'm coming!" Shannon yelled back. She opened the door. "Man, keep it down out here—my downstairs neighbor is probably sleeping."

"I don't care about that old lady. Right now I got a serious problem."

"What happened, and why didn't you use your key?" asked Shannon.

"Shannon, baby, I need you to listen to me," said Xavier. He paced back and forth across her living room.

"What is it, what's going on?" Shannon was beginning to get nervous. She looked out the living-room window. "Where's my car, Xavier?"

"That's what I'm trying to tell you. I went to rob that grocery store on Lake Street and Hennepin. I had the money in my bag when a big-ass guard came out of the bathroom across the hall. He yelled at me and I hit him with my gun and ran past him. I made it outside and was trying to make it to the car when another guard came running at me. They must have called the police, because by the time I got out of the parking lot and hid, they were everywhere.

They're looking for me now. I had to sneak around on the side streets and double back to get here."

"What the hell? So you had to leave my damn car at the place you just robbed?"

"Yes, I didn't have a choice. They were about to catch me, so I had to run."

"You didn't think to park somewhere away from the store? I told you not to ever involve me in your shit!" Shannon yelled. "Now what am I supposed to do? How am I supposed to get my car back?"

"Baby, it will be all right. Just walk up to the store and get the car. When they stop you, just tell them your car was stolen and someone called and told you they saw it," said Xavier, trying to sound calm and in control of the situation.

"You think it will work? I want my car back, but I'm afraid to go up there by myself."

"Ask one of your sisters to take you."

"No, I can't get them involved in this—are you crazy?"

"Then take one of the kids," Xavier suggested. "Yeah, they won't harass you if you have one of them kids with you. Take Lamont with you—they'll be falling all over him, and they won't question you too much."

"No, he's sleeping at Paula's house. I can't believe you just asked me to involve my kids in your shit! I told you I wouldn't do that. *I don't even want to be involved*—but you just put me in your mess. I'll take Teresa to Charlotte's house since it's on the way." *I'm damn sure not leaving with her with Xavier after this shit.* She went to Teresa's room to tell her they were going to Aunt Charlotte's house for a little while.

As they were leaving, Xavier said, "Baby, remember: if they ask about me, tell them you don't know me, do you understand?"

"Of course," Shannon replied. "Now let us go so I can get back home and to bed."

Shannon and her daughter put on their coats and gloves. While it hadn't snowed yet, it was late October and already quite cold. They sang several of Teresa's favorite songs as they walked to Charlotte's house. When they arrived, they went to the side door and Shannon rang the doorbell. No one answered. She knocked hard a few times, but her knocks went unanswered too. They went to the front door and tried again; still no answer. *Shit, now what should I do? I guess we can walk up to the store and see what's going on.*

"Come on, Teresa. No one's home."

"Where are we going now?"

"I need to go to the store."

"Mommy, can I get some candy at the store?" Teresa asked.

"No. I just need to pick something up and then we're going back home."

"But Mommy, I want some candy!" Teresa demanded.

"Teresa, we don't have time for all that. And if the police stop us, don't say anything. Do you hear me?" asked Shannon.

"Yeah," Teresa said with a pout.

"Don't 'yeah' me. I know you know how to talk better than that."

"Yes, Mommy."

When they got to the edge of the parking lot, Shannon saw a lot of police officers there. Two officers stood next to her vehicle as if guarding it. She turned to leave. "Okay, let's go home," she said to Teresa.

"But Mommy, there's our car! We should drive home!" A cop who was standing nearby overheard the girl's innocent outburst.

Oh shit, we gotta get out of here fast. Shannon grabbed Teresa's hand and was about to run when she heard the officer call out, "Ma'am, stop right there!" She turned and saw him running toward them.

All right, here we go. Damn, I can't run with Teresa—they'd catch me for sure.

"Hi. I came to get my car. What's going on?" Shannon asked, approaching the officer.

"What's your name?" The police officer asked.

"Shannon Wilson," she replied. "Is there a problem?"

"This is your vehicle, correct?"

"Uh, it looks like my car, but we walked here, I didn't drive it here," Shannon said.

"The registration says you're the owner. It was involved in a robbery, and we need to ask you a few questions."

Crap, she had to think fast. "Uh, a robbery? When did that happen? I sure hope no one was hurt." *Oh hell, now I'm rambling on and on. I think I'm gonna be sick!*

"I can't tell you that. We're still investigating," the officer replied.

Shannon frowned. "I'm not a suspect, am I?"

"Just a person of interest. It is your car, after all. So if you will come with me ..."

"What about my daughter? Can I call my sister to come get her?"

"Well, that may not be necessary. Let me ask you a couple of questions here. And what's your name, sweetie?" the officer asked as he turned and stooped down to be at eye level with the child.

"Hi, I'm Teresa," she squealed with excitement. "What's your name?"

"My name is Officer Dan." He smiled at the girl and then stood up. "Ms. Wilson, do you know Xavier Hudson?"

"No, I've never heard of him. Is he the person who stole my car?"

"We have reason to suspect it was him. We've been looking for him. He's suspected of being involved on a couple other robberies in the area."

"I don't know him," Shannon said again.

"We know he was coming to your vehicle after he attempted to rob this store. He left the keys in it with the engine running. So, Ms. Wilson, tell me: how do you think he got your keys to your vehicle?"

"Um, well, I don't really know. I noticed my keys were missing after a cookout I went to over Labor Day weekend. I thought I just lost them. I had a spare set at my house."

"So you don't know this Xavier Hudson, never met him, don't have any idea who he is and why he had your car?" asked Officer Dan.

Shannon began to reply. "No, like I sa—"

"I know Xavier, he's my uncle!" Teresa blurted.

"Hush you mouth, Teresa!" Shannon snapped at her daughter.

"Teresa, you said he's your uncle? Do you know where he is?" ask Officer Dan.

"Yessir, he lives at our house," she replied proudly, just like any six-year-old who can answer a question that no one else seems to know the answer to.

"Get a couple of cars over to Miss Wilson's home, now!" the police sergeant ordered the other officers. "And put an APB on Xavier Hudson."

"Miss Wilson, you are under arrest for obstruction of justice and aiding and abetting Xavier Hudson in his commission of numerous robberies in Hennepin County," said Chief Donahue with authority as he closed his handcuffs on Shannon's thin wrists. He continued to read her the Miranda Warning as he led her to a squad car.

"Do you understand these rights as I have stated them to you?"

"Yes, but can you take my daughter to my sister, Charlotte?" she pleaded with the officer.

"No, I'm afraid we have to call Child Protection and they will decide where your child should go."

They took Shannon to the Hennepin County Jail in downtown Minneapolis. Meanwhile, several police went to Shannon's home to arrest Xavier. He was sitting in the living room, drinking a beer and waiting for Shannon to return, when he heard the knock on the door.

"Damn, baby, why didn't you use your key?" he asked as he swung the front door open.

"Xavier Hudson?"

"Naw, he just left about fifteen or twenty minutes ago."

"So who are you then? You look like Xavier," said the officer, taking out a photocopy of Xavier's mug shot from several years ago. "Yeah, I would say you are Xavier Hudson. You are under arrest for the commission of several robberies and attempted robberies." The police pushed their way into the apartment. Several officers grabbed Xavier and put handcuffs on him while another proceeded to check the rest of the home.

The Social Welfare officers took Teresa to a children's center until she could be placed back with her mother or with a relative. As soon as Charlotte, Eddie, and Shannon's other sisters became aware of what had happened, they went to Child Protection trying to seek temporary custody of Teresa and Lamont. They did not want their niece and nephew to be placed into the foster-care system. Charlotte and Eddie retained an attorney and after several weeks of attending hearings and meetings with Social Services and child-protection officers, they were awarded temporary custody of the children.

A few days after the arrest, Shannon entered into a plea bargain with the state in which she would be on probation for two years in exchange for her and Teresa's testimony against Xavier Hudson in the attempted robbery of the grocery store. Just before Thanksgiving, she was released and went to stay with Charlotte and Eddie for a few days. Before being locked up, she had paid her rent for two months in advance and had put money away to cover her bills for at least six months. Now she would have to testify at Xavier's trial; she certainly wouldn't be getting the money she was used to receiving from him.

About a month before the trial date, Shannon and her children moved back into their home. Ever since being released, she couldn't shake the feeling that someone was watching her. At first she thought she was just being paranoid. But the day she returned home, she began receiving calls from Xavier in jail. He knew everything she'd done throughout the day—even told her what she was wearing and whom she'd come in contact with.

"Why do you have someone watching and following me?" Shannon asked.

"I told you before. You can't ever get away from me. I have ways of knowing everything you do. If you start seeing other people, I will hurt you so bad you will wish you were dead."

"You're being ridiculous," she said, laughing. "I just got out of jail because of you. I had my kids taken away and I just got them back. How dare you have someone follow me—and now you're threatening me? I will do what I want. And right now I am going to do whatever it takes for me to get my life back together."

"You better do what I need you to do. You need to make sure you and the kid don't testify at my trial."

"I can't do that. I already went to jail and I am not going to prison for you. That is out of the question!"

"I don't think you understand," Xavier whispered angrily. "I am telling you, not asking you. I suggest you suddenly get a case of severe amnesia. Do not testify, or else something very bad will happen to you. You're going to have me locked up for the rest of my life because you can't keep your mouth shut!"

"Man, you are so fucking stupid and selfish!" Shannon yelled. She hung up on him and then plopped down on her sofa and lit a cigarette.

"Man," Xavier thought aloud, "those broads are gonna have me doing life. They just don't get it. I will have them plugged and they won't even know what's happening."

CHAPTER 17

The next day, Shannon and Lamont put Teresa on her school bus and then walked to Charlotte's house. She couldn't wait to tell her sister about the conversation with Xavier the night before.

"Hi, come on in," Charlotte greeted her sister and nephew.

"Hi, sis. Do you have any clients yet this morning?"

"No, I just finished up one and my next one hasn't arrived yet. She's always late," Charlotte said, rolling her eyes. "Why?"

"Xavier called me last night. He said if me and Teresa testify against him, something bad would happen to us."

"Do you believe him?"

"No, he's just trying to scare me."

"I think he's crazy and would do anything to anyone to stay out of prison. You need to be very careful, Shannon. In fact, if I were you I would let your probation officer know what's going on."

"He's just all talk."

"What? You don't believe he would try to have someone hurt you?" Charlotte asked.

"Oh yeah—can you believe he has someone watching me, too? He told me what I was wearing yesterday and everything I did and where I went." Shannon was trying to keep calm.

"Girl, you need to just pack up and go back to Marion. You know they will hire you back on at RCA." Charlotte pleaded with Shannon. "I am scared for your life and the kids' lives."

"You're overreacting," Shannon said. "He's not that crazy to kill me and my kids. He is always trying to manipulate people, and that's what he's trying to do to me. It won't work. We have to testify and then I move on with my life."

"Well, I hope you're right about all of this," her sister said, "but I wouldn't stay here if I was you. And you need to be even more careful since he has someone watching you. You really need to think about leaving Minnesota."

"We'll be all right. I'll be more cautious now. I wonder who he has watching me?"

"It's probably one of his girls or his hoodlum-ass friends. Please be careful. I'm serious—I don't put anything past him. He is a very dangerous man." Charlotte thought about what Xavier had done to Lee Ann.

"I promise you I will be careful. I love you, Charlotte."

————— ❖ —————

Xavier was very busy at the jail. He kept complaining about his broads and how they were going to get him locked up. He spoke with Jamie frequently, trying to get her to make sure Shannon wouldn't testify against him.

During one of her many visits, Xavier said to her, "Come on, girl, all you have to do is keep her from showing up at my trial."

"I can't do that," Jamie replied. "I would get into big trouble. That's witness tampering or something like that."

"You don't want me to be in the joint for the rest of my life, do you?"

"No, of course not—but I don't want to go to prison, either. I can't go to prison for you."

"You need to do what I tell you to do," Xavier whispered, squeezing her hand underneath the small metal table where they sat. "I have been paying your way for the last few years. If you don't help me, I will hurt you in the worst way."

"Let go of my hand, you're hurting me!" Jamie whispered through clenched teeth. "I'll call the guard over here if you don't."

He loosened his grip. "You better not. You think I'm playing with you, don't you. You need to stop her. I will let you know when and how in a couple of weeks. You have to do as I ask or else you will be the one hurt. I hope you really get what I'm talking about. How's the *baby*?"

Jamie turned as white as a ghost as she began to understand that Xavier was threatening to hurt their baby girl.

She got up to leave, but turned and said, "You're a real bastard, you know that? Threatening to hurt our baby is beyond crazy, even for you!" She turned and walked to the door.

Jamie was terrified of Xavier's threat. She had seen in his eyes that he meant what he'd said. When she reached her car, the tears began flowing. She couldn't believe what he had just told her—and the way he'd squeezed her hand so tight, it was still throbbing.

She didn't know what to do. She couldn't go back in there and tell the guards what had just happened. She would go home and wait a few days to see what his next move would be. She was so scared she had a hard time focusing on driving home. She ran a stop sign and almost hit a car in the intersection. Jamie pulled over to the side of the road and smoked a cigarette to try to calm down. She would act as though he hadn't said anything to her and go about her regular routines. But even as she thought about it, she knew that Xavier would be contacting her soon.

CHAPTER 18

Shannon and her kids got up early to see and open all the gifts Santa Claus had brought for the children. After playing with their presents and eating a light breakfast, they bathed and dressed and went to celebrate Christmas at Charlotte and Eddie's house. Other family members came through after having their own celebrations.

It was so nice to be with family and close friends after all Shannon had been through. There was plenty of food; everyone brought a dish to share and desserts were in abundance. She enjoyed watching her kids playing with their cousins while the adults listened to music, talked, and drank adult beverages. She was especially happy her mom and dad had been able to come for a visit for the holidays. This was one of the most special and blessed Christmases she could remember. Everything was just perfect.

Xavier continued to call her many times a day, still trying to harass and manipulate her into not testifying. She didn't always answer the phone. She thought about returning to Marion, as Charlotte had suggested. Paula had begged her to not get involved with Xavier from the beginning, and she'd often told Shannon how much she despised him. Her sister Regina hadn't approved of her dating Xavier either. She thought back to all the advice from her family and friends who loved her most; she'd been too blind to see him for what he really was. *Oh well. I have to deal with the courts now; I can't run, for my kids' sake. I have to deal with this and testify at his trial. Then and only then will I ever be able to get on with my life.* Shannon watched the snow falling outside her living-room window.

For New Year's Eve, Shannon and a lot of her family and friends all went to a party at a fancy hotel in downtown Minneapolis. They had a great time ringing in the new year. They ate, danced, and drank until the wee hours of the morning. Shannon went home and slept until two in the afternoon. Lying in bed, she thought about how much fun they'd all had the night before; she'd even met a couple of guys who gave her their phone numbers. She didn't know if she would call them before she testified at the trial, but she felt happy to have met some new people. She got out of the bed, showered, grabbed a sandwich, and headed out the door to pick up her kids at Charlotte's house.

She stayed a little while talking with Charlotte and Eddie. "So are you ready for the trial?" Eddie asked.

"As ready as I'll ever be. It should be easy for me. I meet with my attorney and the state attorney again next week. They already recorded me and Teresa answering the state attorney's questions. I really don't know a whole lot of details about what Xavier was doing. I don't even know all the places he robbed. And remember, I thought he was in banking and owned several businesses."

"Yeah, that's right, you did believe everything he told you," said Charlotte. "Even when we tried to tell your ass all about him when we found out he was the same asshole who married Lee Ann. Well, when this is all over, you can make a fresh start of your life here. Everything will be just fine."

"Yes, it will," added Eddie. "You just have to realize—when it seems like your family's only telling you the bad stuff, it's because we don't want you to go through crap like this."

"I do see that now. And I will listen to all of your advice going forward. I'm going to notify my attorney of Xavier's threats. I love all of you. Thank you so much for all you've done for me and my kids. They love you both so much." Shannon smiled. "Now I need to get going. I want to cook and then relax and enjoy some special time with Teresa and Lamont." She stood and gave Eddie and Charlotte each a hug, and then called her kids to come get their coats on.

As they walked to the car, Shannon had a weird sense that they were being watched. She quickly put the kids into the backseat. As she went around to the driver's side, she saw someone standing next to a tree in the neighbor's yard across the street. The person was dressed all in black and seemed to be a woman. Shannon quickly got in the car, locked all the doors, and drove off. In the rearview mirror she could see the person standing in the middle of the street, watching her go. She wasn't sure, but she thought it looked like Lee Ann!

Shannon took the long way home in case someone was following her. When she pulled up in front of her house, she looked at all the surroundings, feeling scared that someone might be watching her house. Only when she felt sure no one was out there did she get the kids out of the car and walk them up to the house. Once inside, she immediately locked the door and made sure all of the windows were locked. She even checked the bathroom and every closet. Only then could she feel safe in her home.

Shannon turned on the television and called the kids to come in the living room so they would all be in the same room. After a while, she felt calm enough to cook dinner and relax. They spent the evening watching television together. The kids fell asleep around ten o'clock; she woke Teresa and helped her get in bed, and then she carried Lamont and put him in his crib.

Peeking out of a living-room window, Shannon saw the same person standing across the street, staring up at her. She went to call Charlotte and Eddie to tell them what was going on. She took one more look out the window, but the person was gone. She called Charlotte anyway.

"Girl, why didn't you call me right when you got home?" said Charlotte. "We would have come by for a while and checked things out. You already know Xavier has someone watching you, and he definitely doesn't want you to show up to the hearing."

"I know, I meant to call you when I got home, but no one was watching me when we got here. I went through the house and made sure no one had got in. We watched TV for a while and I didn't think about it until I put the kids to bed."

"Do you want me and Eddie to come over now?"

"No, I just looked out the window again and I didn't see anyone."

"Does she know who the person is?" Shannon heard Eddie asking in the background.

"I'm not sure, but she looked like Lee Ann," replied Shannon. She heard Charlotte repeating the information to Eddie.

"That's it," said Eddie, "we are coming over."

"No, you don't have to come out. It's real cold. I'm fine; I only called to let you know what I saw."

Eddie had grabbed the phone from Charlotte. "Okay, but if anything else happens or if she comes back, call us right away."

"Okay, I will. Bye for now."

"Bye," Eddie said. After he'd hung up, he said to Charlotte, "Come on, let's go."

"Go where?" Charlotte asked, already getting up to put on her coat and boots.

"You know. I just had to get her off the phone. You know how stubborn you Wilson girls can be; I would've been on the phone all night, going back and forth. We don't have to go in—I just want to check things out." Eddie put on his coat and grabbed his gun.

As Eddie turned the car onto Shannon's block, he noticed a lady dressed in black across the street, looking up at the front of Shannon's home. It was definitely his cousin Lee Ann. He turned off the headlights and quickly pulled over. He got out of the car and quietly walked behind where Lee Ann was standing. Charlotte started to tell him not to go, but then she too saw Lee Ann. Eddie didn't make any sound except the light crunching of snow under his feet. Lee Ann seemed not to hear him.

"Lee Ann, what are you doing here?" he asked.

"Oh my God! You scared me to death!" she exclaimed after catching her breath.

"Answer me, damn it!" Eddie yelled at his cousin. "Are you the one who's been watching Shannon and telling that asshole husband of yours everything she does? That is so sick! Why would you do that?"

"He just asked me to do it. It's not like I'm gonna hurt her or anything. I was just watching her for him."

"But why would you do that after everything that bastard has done to you? He almost killed you! Do you want him to hurt Shannon or worse? I just don't understand you."

Eddie paced in a circle, trying to calm himself down. Charlotte had moved the car and parked in front of Shannon's. She jumped out and ran across the street to where Eddie and Lee Ann were standing.

"What the hell?" Charlotte said. "It's *you*? You've been following my sister around? Why?" Charlotte grabbed Lee Ann by the coat and shook her.

By now, Shannon had heard the commotion, seen them all through her living-room window, and went outside. "What's going on? I told you not to come over."

"I'll explain all of that later," said Charlotte, letting go of Lee Ann's collar. "Right now we're waiting for Lee Ann to tell us why she's been following you and reporting back to Xavier. Well, Lee Ann? We're waiting."

"Well, he's my husband and I love him. He asked me to just watch and let him know everything Shannon did, what she wore each day, and who she's spending time with." Lee Ann was looking down at the ground. She didn't see Shannon's punch coming. It hit Lee Ann square on the jaw, and then Shannon tackled her to the ground.

Shannon sat on top of Lee Ann, yelling in her face. "You can have Xavier, because I am done with him. But bitch, you *better* stay away from me and my kids! If you don't, I will fucking kill you! I have never done anything to you—and everyone told me you and Xavier weren't together!"

"But—" Lee Ann started to speak.

"Don't say another word, Lee Ann, or I will kick your ass myself," Eddie interrupted.

"Leave here," Shannon said, "and don't let me ever catch you spying on me. You are the craziest woman I have ever met." She and Charlotte crossed the street back to her house.

Eddie looked at his cousin, realizing how crazy she was. "I can't believe you would do this shit for that no-good nigga. You know firsthand he's a real bad person—and yet you would help him try and hurt another person? What the hell is wrong with you? Get the hell out of here—you disgust me!"

Shannon, Charlotte, and Eddie sat in Shannon's kitchen, drinking beers and discussing what had just happened. Eddie was shocked and embarrassed by his cousin's behavior. He couldn't believe she would do this for that motherfucker. He was so mad he wanted to smack his cousin around a bit—though he knew he wouldn't do any such thing. They agreed that although Lee Ann might be crazy about Xavier, she seemed harmless overall. They felt that Shannon was going to be safe.

She continued to receive calls from Xavier at least twice a week, but he had stopped asking her not to testify, and he'd stopped threatening her and Teresa. He began talking nice, not bringing up the trial at all. And he stopped telling her what she'd been wearing and doing each day. While Shannon noticed the sudden change, she was mostly relieved about it. Xavier would talk about the fun times they'd had together in the early months of their relationship.

Shannon knew they would never be together again. She felt comfortable talking with Xavier on the phone, knowing he was locked up and knowing that they would never again be anything more than friends.

She didn't know that Xavier was still talking about her every day with Jamie, Lee Ann, and others. He complained constantly to other inmates about all three of the women and how they were trying to keep him locked up. The closer it got to his trial date, the more anxious he grew to stop anyone from testifying against him. He knew he would make all of them pay.

On January 12, 1978, Jamie visited Xavier once again at the Hennepin County Jail. This time she brought their baby to the visit. It started pleasantly; Jamie was glad she'd come to see him. After all, she loved Xavier and they had a baby together. They talked and held hands as he played with the baby on his lap. Then he turned to Jamie, saying he had to tell her something very important.

"I need you to go to this girl's house and spend the night at her place with her and her two kids," he said.

"What? But why do you want me to do that?" asked Jamie.

"Just listen to me," he said, getting impatient with her for asking questions. She could see his demeanor was changing; he was now glaring at her whenever the guards weren't paying attention. She started to get a bad vibe from him.

"You love me and want me to be with you and the baby, right?" She nodded. She knew he was going to once again ask her to hurt the woman.

"You have to get some gas before you go over there," Xavier whispered. "After she goes to bed, you need to set the house on fire. Burn it down to the ground. If you don't do it, they are going to put me away for a long time, until I'm too old to do anything. I know you don't want me to be away from you for so many years, right? I won't see our baby grow up and we won't be together again." *Come on, you stupid broad*, Xavier thought to himself, *just do it.*

"I can't do anything like that, I told you before. I can't hurt anyone—especially children!" She was talking a little too loud for Xavier's liking.

"If you don't lower your voice I will beat you right here in front of these guards. Now, make sure you are listening real carefully to what I'm about to tell you. Are you listening? If you don't do it, I will have someone kill our baby. It may not be right away, but it will happen, I promise you—and you will have her blood on your hands for the rest of your life. In fact, if you don't tell me right now that you're in, I will snap the baby's neck right here." Xavier tightened his arm around the baby. "Don't fucking test me, Jamie. I don't have anything else to lose at this point."

Tears ran down Jamie's cheeks as she grabbed for her baby. "Yes, I'll do it," she said, and Xavier released the baby to her.

"Fantastic! That's all I needed to hear. Now, I will set it all up and I'll call you tomorrow with the details. Wasn't that nice and easy?" He smiled at her.

"Uh, I gotta go now. The baby's getting tired."

"Remember to do as I say and keep your mouth shut about it," he warned her as he kissed one cheek and wiped the tears off the other cheek. Jamie left the jail, determined that she would not have her baby harmed or killed because this woman was going to testify. She didn't know what choice she had except to do as he asked.

Shannon received a call from Xavier later that night. He explained to her that an inmate friend of his needed help for his wife and baby. Their apartment had caught on fire, and she needed a place to stay for a few days. He told her the girl would come over the next night, and she should let her and the baby stay as long as they needed. Shannon, having a big heart; of course agreed right away. She never gave it a second thought.

Xavier also called Jamie to go over the plan again. She would go to Shannon's house pretending that her apartment had caught on fire and she needed a place to stay for a few days. She should tell Shannon that her husband was in jail with Xavier. Once Shannon and the kids were sleeping, she was to douse the place with gasoline and light it on fire. He didn't tell her he was also making other arrangements, just in case Jamie didn't go through with it.

That night, around nine o'clock, Jamie put her baby in her yellow Volkswagen and drove to the address Xavier had given her. Instead of taking the gas with her to the woman's home, she had taken it back to her apartment and put it in a storage shed. She arrived around nine-thirty and carried her baby and a diaper bag up the stairs to Shannon's apartment. She knocked on Shannon's door, trying to calm herself down. She hoped Shannon wouldn't be home—but a few moments later, Shannon opened the door. "Hi, you must be Jamie."

"Uh, yes, I am—and this is Abigail. Thank you so much for letting us stay with you for a few days. I hate to be a bother."

"Oh, it's no bother. Come in out of the cold. Here, let me help you with your bag."

"Thank you." Once inside, Jamie took a blanket from the bag and laid it out on the floor. She set the baby on it, hoping she would soon go to sleep. She glanced around the home, trying to see if Shannon's kids were there; just then they came running from a room at the back of the apartment.

"Xavier told me your apartment caught on fire. I'm just glad you and Abigail were able to get out safely."

"Uh, yeah, thanks. I really appreciate you helping us."

Teresa sat next to Jamie on the couch. Shannon and Jamie drank beer and talked about their kids, watching television with Teresa and Lamont. Jamie was still extremely nervous, so she tried to keep talking.

After a while, Jamie got up to use the bathroom. She splashed water on her face to try to get herself together. She stood looking at her reflection in the medicine-cabinet mirror, silently asking herself what she was doing here. She had wondered about Shannon and Xavier's relationship. She opened the cabinet door to see if there was any aspirin. There was, along with men's shaving cream, aftershave, deodorant, soap—all in the same brands that Xavier had brought to Jamie's own apartment. There was even the same kind of razor that Xavier used. *I guess I have my answer*, Jamie thought. *That two-timing bastard*. She glanced at her reflection once more before exiting the bathroom.

After the kids went to bed, Shannon and Jamie watched TV until about eleven o'clock. After Shannon finally turned in, Jamie waited until midnight to make sure the other woman was sleeping. She grabbed her baby and ran out of the house, leaving all the formula and diapers in the diaper bag next to the couch. She got the baby in the car and headed back to her apartment. *Shannon and her kids are so nice, I just can't kill them.*

CHAPTER 19

When Shannon woke up the next morning, she entered her living room quietly, trying not to disturb Jamie and the baby. She was surprised to find that they weren't there, but that the diaper bag was still sitting on the floor. She looked in the kitchen, but it too was vacant. She heard someone in the living room, but it was Teresa.

"Mommy, where's the lady and her baby?" asked Teresa. "Did they go home?"

"I don't know, honey, they were already gone when I got up."

"But Mommy, she forgot to take the baby's stuff." Teresa picked up the bag and opened it. "It still has the baby's milk and bottles and diapers, Mommy. Won't the baby need her stuff?"

"Yes, she probably will. I wonder why she just up and left like that. Oh well, maybe she just wasn't comfortable here," Shannon said, more to herself than to her daughter.

Later that day, Paula stopped by to see how they were doing. Shannon was glad to see her. She told Paula all about the bizarre Lee Ann who'd been watching her all this time. And how the girl from last night just up and left in the middle of the night, so fast that she left her baby's formula and diapers.

"Well, it's not surprising to me," Paula said. "They are both connected to Xavier. I am a bit surprised you would let a complete stranger come in your house, though."

"I know. I probably shouldn't have. I just felt sorry for her because she lost her home in a fire and she and her baby needed somewhere to stay."

"I understand that, but that chick could have tried to hurt you. And with Lee Ann acting crazy, running around spying on folks, you need to be extra careful. What is with these damn fool women and Xavier? They all act like they ain't got no damn sense."

"But what if she and that beautiful little baby really did need a place to stay? That would have been awful of me to turn them away," Shannon said.

"Yeah, that's true. But don't let just anyone up in here anymore."

"I won't," Shannon promised. "What are you doing tonight? I was thinking about going to see that new movie *Saturday Night Fever*. I heard it's real good. Or we can see something else if you want to—I just want to get out of this house."

"What time are you going?" asked Paula.

"Let me call Rhonda and see if she can watch the kids for me. We can take my car."

"No, we'll take my car. After everything that's happened lately, I don't want to be in your car!" Paula let out a nervous chuckle.

"Okay, I can't blame you for that. I'll be right back." Shannon went in her bedroom to call her sister Rhonda. When she returned to the living room, Paula was looking out of the window.

"I'm ready. Rhonda is at the salon, but she said to bring them over there. Hey, are you all right?"

"Yes, I was just thinking: what if Xavier had sent that woman over here to kill you? Have you thought about that?" Paula asked with a shiver.

"Yes, but not until afterward, when I think about the way she left. But she was so mousy looking and soft-spoken, I don't think she could hurt a fly. Let's just go and enjoy ourselves; I don't want to talk or think about it right now."

They went to the movies and had a relaxing night. Afterward they stopped to pick up some dinner before picking up the kids; they all went back to eat at Shannon's house. When Paula parked the car, they saw a shadowy figure across the street, startling both of them.

The figure started walking toward a car, and they were relieved to see that it was only a neighbor being picked up in front of his house.

Xavier called Jamie on the following Saturday. He was anxious to hear if she'd done what he had asked her. He hadn't heard anything about the fire on the news.

"So what happened? Did you take care of it?" he demanded to know.

"No," Jamie said. "There is no way I could kill a woman and her two babies."

Xavier was furious. He wished she were in front of him so he could wring her damn neck. "I don't want to argue about this with you!" he yelled in the phone and hung up on her. He had to put his backup plan in place fast.

He had been befriending a white boy named Dean Olmstead. Dean had become an inmate at the Hennepin County Jail about thirty days after Xavier had arrived there.

"What are you in for?" Xavier had asked Dean.

"Why do you want to know?" Dean replied.

"You don't look like you'd do anything major. So what'd you do? Forget to pay some parking tickets?" Xavier pushed further.

"No—I killed someone during a robbery. I did my time, but I violated my probation, so here I am. What about you?"

"Armed robbery," Xavier told him.

Dean's probation had required him to obtain and maintain employment. He was also ordered to do community service and pay hefty court fees and fines of restitution from a breaking-and-entering charge from the prior year. He hadn't fulfilled the court order and probation requirements, so he was arrested by his probation officer. When they met, he was serving sixty days.

Xavier began sharing his meals with Dean and looking out for him. They were often seen sitting on their bunks, talking to each other all night. Dean saw Xavier as a friend who always had a protective watch over him.

About two weeks before Dean was to be released, Xavier told him that he might need him to do something real important—something that would save Xavier from spending a major portion of the rest of his life in prison. They were sitting at a table next to a wall in the common room. Xavier reminded Dean about the situation he was in and how his girl Shannon had signed an agreement to testify against him back in November.

<hr>

"Man, I can't get this broad to understand she can't testify against me," Xavier told Dean. "She is really killing me, man. And then my other girl Jamie won't help solve my problem. She's so scared of everything. Man, I even told her I would have our baby killed if she didn't help me. You'd think that would get a bitch moving to do whatever she needed to do to protect the kid. Not her, man—she still too scared to help me out."

"I hear ya, but what do you need me to do?" asked Dean.

"My trial was supposed to be in December, but now it's been moved to the end of January. If my girl Jamie doesn't come through on this, I need you to help me out. I need you to catch Shannon's apartment on fire with her and the kids in it."

"Damn, man, I don't know about that. Now all I do is simple breaking-and-entering stuff—and that's only when I can't hold down a job." Dean paused. "What will I get out of it?"

"I'll have Jamie meet you the day you get released. She'll give you a thousand dollars—and her dad owns a business and she can get you a good job with the company."

"I need to think about this one. I'll let you know a few days before I get out," Dean said, pondering the proposition.

"Okay. It's real important for me. While you're thinking it over, remember how much I've done for you while you've been here. Also, you know I can get to you, too, from in here." Xavier got up from the table and walked away, leaving Dean sitting stunned and confused.

On January 16, Dean met up with Xavier again. "So did it happen yet?" he asked.

"No, the silly broad still says she can't do it," said Xavier.

"You're sure she'll meet me here and give me the money as soon as I walk out those doors? And I will definitely get a job at her dad's company?" asked Dean.

"Yeah—and if all goes well, I'll even have her give you another two thousand." Xavier was really anxious now. "I gotta have this small problem taken care of as soon as you get out."

"Are you *sure* she will do this part, knowing what's about to happen?" Dean needed reassurance. He was scared as hell to do something like this. But the money and a job—rather a damn good job—were pushing him to do it.

"Yeah, she will do this. She just couldn't do the final deed herself." Xavier was so elated about this turn of events in his favor that he could barely contain his excitement. He explained to Dean how it would go down.

"Jamie already has two of those two-gallon gas cans filled with gasoline. The day you get out, she'll meet you outside the jail here. At night, she'll pick you up and drive you to Shannon's house. You go to the door and push your way in. You will have to restrain them somehow so they don't get out of the apartment. Whatever you do, make sure you get the little girl, because if she somehow survives she will run her mouth—and you'll be right back in here with me. Get in, do the job, and get out. It has to be quick because once the gas catches the fire, it's gonna spread fast. It will be the most intense hotness you've ever seen and felt. Don't get caught up in it—it will be so mesmerizing, almost hypnotizing. After that, Jamie will drive you out of there and you need to lie low. You can't make any mistakes or else we're all going down."

"I got it. And she'll have the thousand up front, right?"

"Yeah, I already told you she would. She'll be here visiting me, and when you're released, she will be waiting for you."

"Okay, I won't let you down," said Dean.

You better not, if you want to live long, white boy. Xavier smiled and winked at Dean.

Xavier called Jamie that night and told her she needed to come see him on the morning of January 19. He told her the plan was moving forward and that she should get $1,000 out of their stash and bring it with her but leave it in the car until after her visit. Jamie showed up on January 19 as she'd been told to. During the visit, Xavier gave her all of the details about how everything was to go down. He'd told Dean to walk past the visiting area so she could get a look at him.

Jamie repeated the plan to make sure she had it right. "I just have to give him the money, then pick him up later at his girlfriend's apartment, drive him to the other place, and then take him to his friend's apartment when it's done. I don't have to go inside and help him, right?"

"Yes, that's all. Wait in the visitors' area and I'll have someone give you a message. At that time you should leave and go over to the courthouse across the street to meet him. Then go home and I'll call you again later this evening. Do you understand?" Xavier asked.

About an hour after Jamie left the visiting room, Xavier received a message from another inmate on Dean's behalf. "He said to tell you 'I'm going to court and I'll be getting out after court and I'll take care of it,'" the inmate relayed to Xavier.

"Thanks for the message, man," Xavier said. He turned toward another inmate who had a visitor and signaled for him to have his girl tell Jamie to do as planned.

Later on that day, Xavier called Shannon. He was trying to see if she'd be home that night. They talked for a few minutes until he found out she was planning on being home. He said he had to get going but he would try to call her later.

One of Shannon's brothers came to borrow her car late that afternoon. She didn't mind letting her family use her car after Teresa was home from school and if she wasn't going anywhere. She loved her brother and he didn't ask for it very often.

"I should be back no later than nine tonight," Adrian said. "I may even be back before that."

"Okay, I'll be here," Shannon replied. They talked for a while before he left. He thanked her and gave her a hug.

Shannon watched some TV as she filled out job applications for various companies in Minneapolis and St. Paul. She wanted to have them ready to turn in after her part of the trial was finished. At around five o'clock, she fixed dinner for herself and the kids. She then helped Teresa with her homework and gave the kids their baths. They watched television together until it was time for the children to go to bed. Then she called Paula and talked to her for a while.

Earlier that afternoon, Jamie had met Dean at the courthouse as planned. When she approached him, a woman who appeared to be his girlfriend and a couple of other friends were with him.

"Are you Dean Olmstead?" she asked as she approached the group. "I'm Jamie Lincoln."

"Yeah, I'm Dean, Xavier's friend."

"I need to talk to Dean for a few minutes," she said to the girlfriend as they stepped a few feet away from the group.

"Here," she said, discreetly handing him the money, which was wrapped in a handkerchief. "What's the address so I can pick you up tonight?"

"Here it is," Dean said, taking a piece of paper from his pocket and handing it to her.

"Okay, good. I'll pick you up around eight. Xavier said we need to be there by nine."

"Good, good," Dean said. To his girlfriend, he explained, "I'm going to burn some clothes for Xavier. She's going to take me to pick them up."

Jamie had already turned and was walking back to her car. She was a nervous wreck. She lit a cigarette even before she started the engine. She wanted this to all be over.

She went to her apartment and tried to eat a little. She had no appetite, though, so she watched TV and tried to get some rest. She wasn't able to sleep. At about six forty-five she got up, washed her face, got her shoes on, and went to the storage shed to load the two gas cans into the trunk of her car. At seven o'clock she left her apartment and drove to the address Dean had given her. She arrived around seven thirty. Dean was waiting for her, dressed in jeans and a down jacket; he had a ski mask on, although the mask wasn't pulled down over his face.

They didn't talk much on the drive into Minneapolis to Shannon's home.

"Did you bring the gas?" Dean asked.

"Yeah," Jamie replied. They drove the rest of the way with the radio on, not speaking. They arrived at Shannon's house ten minutes before nine o'clock. Jamie parked the car in front of a house down the street from Shannon's and turned off the lights but left the engine running.

"Where's the gas?" Dean asked.

"It's in the trunk."

Dean got out of the car and retrieved the gas from the trunk. He quickly went up to Shannon's door and set the gas behind him before he knocked on the door. Shannon answered, thinking it was Adrian returning her car. She opened the door and saw a man she didn't know.

Shannon tried to slam the door, but the man pushed his way in. She tried to run from him, but he was right behind her. He grabbed a vase from a table near the doorway and hit her on the back of the head. She was losing consciousness.

"Xavi—"

She blacked out completely. He quickly pulled her body farther inside the living room and grabbed the gas cans, shutting and locking the front door. He moved her to what seemed to be her bedroom and laid her on the bed. He used wire to tie her hands and feet to the bed rails and stuffed a gag in her mouth, taping it shut. She was coming to just as he secured the tape. Next he went into the hallway and found the other bedroom, where a little girl was asleep in her bed and a baby boy slept in a crib. He quickly placed a cloth in the girl's mouth to gag her as well, and then tied her hands and feet to the bed; the baby boy slept through it all. He ran to the living room and grabbed the gas cans. He set one inside the woman's bedroom and carried the other to the kids' room.

Shannon came to and was trying desperately to free herself when she heard a knock on the front door. She tried to scream, but the cloth in her mouth muffled any noise trying to escape her throat. She could hear Teresa trying to do the same. She began to cry.

Adrian arrived at Shannon's house at about fifteen minutes after nine. He knocked on the door, but she didn't answer. He waited a few minutes, wondering where she could be. She had to be home, because he had her car. He knocked a few more times and waited a couple more minutes. He called out to her through the door.

"Shannon, it's Adrian. Are you here? Come on, Shannon it's freezing out here," he said, getting annoyed.

He knocked several more times and then went downstairs to see if the elderly lady was home so he could ask if she'd seen Shannon and the children. He knocked several times on the neighbor's door; no answer there, either. Adrian went back upstairs and pounded on Shannon's door. *BAM BAM BAM!* Nothing.

That girl sure sleeps real deep, he thought. He looked at Shannon's keychain; no house key. He tried one more time. *I guess I'll have to come back in a little bit,* he thought, turning to go back to the car.

Shannon heard her brother pleading for her to answer the door. She couldn't open the door even though she desired to do so with every fiber of her body. She wanted to scream for Adrian's help, but she knew he couldn't hear her. Teresa heard her uncle too but was just as helpless. Shannon finally realized that Xavier was really going to have her and her babies killed. He'd sent this man to kill them. Paula's words filled her head: *Be extra careful and don't let strangers in your home. Do you think that girl was really here to hurt you?* She also heard all of the advice and warnings her sisters and brothers had tried to give her about Xavier. Then she heard her brother leaving down the steps. It was all too late.

Dean heard Adrian leaving also. He began pouring the gasoline all over Shannon's body, from her hair down to her feet. He doused the carpet and furniture closest to the bed upon which she lay bound and helpless. Next he went back to the children's room and poured gas all over Teresa. She screamed as the fumes and fluid raced into her eyes and nose and made her skin burn. Dean tried to block out their piercing screeches as he continued to douse the kids' bedroom. The baby boy was fully awake and crying, screaming for his mommy. Dean went back into Shannon's room to retrieve the other gas can. He walked back to Teresa and stared down at her pleading eyes as tears streamed down her beautiful cheeks. He studied her eyes and mouth for a short moment. Without saying a word, he placed the gas can, which was still two-thirds full, between her knees. Next he took some wire and tied it to the can, then strung it under her body and around a finger on her left hand. He turned to the screaming baby, removed him from the crib, and let him crawl on the gas-soaked carpet. He took the book of matches and struck one; he threw it onto the girl's bed and watched for a second as the bed was engulfed in flames. He quickly lit a couple more matches and threw them to various areas of the room. He ran to Shannon's room and struck a match and threw it on her body. He could hear their agonizing screams even through the gags. He heard the beds moving as they flung their bodies from side to side, trying desperately to escape the flames.

Dean ran out the front door, down the steps, and toward Jamie's car. His pant leg was on fire and he was patting it as he ran. Feathers left a long trail as they fell from his down coat, which had melted in several places from the heat of the flames.

"Let's go!" he yelled as he got into the car. Jamie sped off.

A man walking past saw Dean running from the house and get into a yellow Volkswagen. He heard a loud noise come from Shannon's house and looked up to see the top floor of the duplex in flames. He ran to the nearest house and banged on the front door. He asked a teenage boy who answered the door to call the fire department. The fire trucks arrived within five minutes.

Adrian turned onto the street, returning to see if Shannon was home or awake yet. The street was blocked off, so he left the car in the middle of the street and ran as fast as he could toward Shannon's house. Two policemen stopped him. "Sir, you can't go up there!" one of the officers told him.

"I have to, my sister and her two kids live on the top floor! God, they have to be okay!" Adrian began to sob hysterically. "Where are they? Did you get them out?"

"Sir, what's your name?"

"Adrian Wilson. Are Shannon and the kids at the hospital? Please tell me where they are!"

"Mr. Wilson, we haven't been able to get inside yet. They're doing everything they can to put the fire out so we can get in there. No one has seen Miss Wilson or her children," the officer said. "Are you sure she was home?"

"Yes, I think so. I borrowed her car and I told her I'd be back by nine. I was here less than an hour ago to return the car, but she didn't answer the door. I knocked and knocked. I even went downstairs to see if the neighbor had seen her. She didn't answer either. I should have stayed! God, I should have stayed." Adrian collapsed to his knees on the hard snow and screamed with agony, crying and crying until he threw up in the snow. After a while he stood up and told the officer who remained by his side that he needed to call the rest of their family. "Someone has to tell them. Can you call them?"

"Yes. Can you give me a couple of their phone numbers? I'll have someone notify them right away," said the officer.

"I can't believe this is really happening," said Adrian. He wrote down Charlotte's phone number and gave it to the officer. The officer took Adrian over to the police car so he could get out of the cold. He then radioed in to his precinct to have the family notified.

Soon after, Charlotte, Eddie, Regina, and Paula arrived at the fire. They were all hysterical. When Adrian saw them, he got out of the squad car and ran to hug them. They all stood in disbelief, watching the flames reaching into the air from the house, which no longer had a roof. They watched the firemen working hard to put out the fire. It burned so intensely the onlookers could feel the heat from across the street. The flames shot out from the house in blue, orange, red, and yellow. In some spots it was so hot it burned in a purplish hue.

"Come on, men," yelled the fire captain, "we've got to get this under control!"

"It's not responding in some spots," one of the firefighters replied. "We get part of it out and it starts to flame up on us again."

"It must be a gas fire. Did the gas company turn off the gas off to the house yet?"

"Yes, both the gas and electricity have been cut off to both apartments. I think an accelerant of some type may have been used."

"Damn it, in that case we'll have to let it burn off for a while before the water will put it all the way out. Make sure those flames don't spread to the other houses!"

They worked on the fire for at least forty-five minutes before it was finally completely extinguished. Meanwhile, other family members, friends, and neighbors arrived and waited in shock. All the local television and newspaper reporters were already on the scene.

After the fire was put out and had cooled down enough, the fire chief and his team of investigators went in and began the task of looking for bodies and evidence of what had caused the fire. They began on the ground floor, at the neighbor's home in the front of the house, and worked toward the back. Their first task was to see if there was anyone in the house. They didn't find any bodies in the bottom apartment, so they moved on to what remained of the second floor. They called out in case anyone had miraculously survived the fire. When the chief entered what used to be the first bedroom, he saw Shannon's charred body bound to the bed by her wrists and feet.

"Oh dear God," he muttered as he looked at the charred body. As he moved closer he could smell a strong odor of gasoline and could see something binding the corpse to the bed.

"Hey, go notify the police outside—this is a homicide," ordered the chief. The others moved to the second bedroom, where they saw the body of what appeared to be a toddler lying partially under a bed upon which the body of an older child was bound with wire around its wrists; a gas can had been placed between the child's knees.

"Oh, Mary Mother of God!" a rookie firefighter exclaimed as he covered his mouth and took in the horrible scene before him. He ran out the back door, where he began retching over the rail at the top of the stairs.

The firemen left the house and the police homicide detectives and forensics team took over. Some of the police officers bagged the trail of feathers that began at the front door of the top apartment and led down the stairs and sidewalk to the front of the next house on the street. They waited for the coroners to arrive before they touched the bodies. The bodies weren't removed from the house until close to midnight.

"Why would anyone do this," the police chief said. "Those babies didn't deserve this. And to bind someone to a bed, pour gasoline on them, and light them on fire—that's the most inhumane act anyone could do. Whoever did this is an animal with no conscience. We've got to get this bastard!"

The night after the murders, Paula and Shannon's sister Regina left Regina's house to go for a drive. They'd gone about six blocks when another car came up behind them and began flashing its high beams on and off.

"What the hell is that car doing? He keeps flashing his bright lights on and off and he keeps getting real close to us," Regina said.

"Don't stop—keep driving and see what they do," said Paula.

"Okay, I'm going to turn at the next block to see if they follow us." Regina drove to the next block and made a right turn. The other car followed.

"I'm going back to my house. It could be the same person who killed Shannon and the kids," Regina said. Suddenly, red and blue police lights lit up on top of the other car. Regina continued to drive home. The officer blared the sirens a couple of times trying to get them to pull over, but Regina refused to stop until she reached the front of her apartment building. Once she finally came to a stop, two officers got out of their car and began yelling at Regina.

"What's your name? Give me your driver's license. Why didn't you pull over when I signaled to you?" the first office demanded.

"My name is Regina Wilson. You flashed your bright lights on and off at me. I didn't know who the hell you were. You should have turned your police lights on to begin with," said Regina as she retrieved her driver's license from her purse and handed it to the officer.

"When an officer signals you to pull over, you have to stop. Why are you so afraid of the police? Are you hiding something in your car?" asked the second officer.

"No, you asshole, my cousin—her sister," Paula said, gesturing to Regina, "and her two children were murdered last night. We didn't know if you were the murderers or what. Leave us the fuck alone. There may have been a lot of people involved, maybe even some crooked cops."

"Oh, shit," the officer said. "I'm sorry about your family. But make sure you stop the next time an officer signals for you to pull over. We'll catch the people who murdered your family. And rest assured, it's highly unlikely any officers were involved. Go on in the house; I'll make sure you get in safely." They all walked to the front door, and the officers waited until the women were in and they heard the door lock before returning to their car.

"Oh man, that's terrible," said the first office. "We tried to pull over the family of that poor woman who was murdered in that fire last night."

"Yeah. I didn't want to say anything," the second officer said, "but I heard they arrested the bastards who did it earlier today. I see why they were so scared—those murders were brutal." The policemen got into their patrol car and drove away.

For months afterward, Regina and Paula and most of their family lived in fear.

EPILOGUE

Shannon's family told the police about Teresa telling officers where Xavier was living and that Shannon and Teresa were supposed to testify at his trial for a string of robberies he'd committed. They told the police how Xavier had had someone following Shannon for the past two months and how he had threatened to kill her if she went through with testifying. They also told the police about Jamie.

Working on a tip from a neighbor, the homicide detectives were able trace a yellow Volkswagen to Jamie Lincoln. They linked her to Xavier Hudson, as she had visited him frequently while he was being held awaiting his trial. From all the evidence at the fire, the information from the family, and police records, the detectives were able to link Shannon to Xavier, and then Xavier to Jamie and Dean. On the afternoon of January 20, 1978, Jamie Lincoln was arrested in connection with the murders of Shannon, Teresa, and Lamont Wilson. Jamie led police to Dean Olmstead, who was arrested that same night for the murders of Shannon, Teresa, and Lamont Wilson. They brought charges against Xavier Hudson the next morning, also for the murders of Shannon, Teresa, and Lamont Wilson.

The family had to put their grief on hold as they had to plan the funerals for Shannon and her children. It was very difficult; most of them felt some guilt and were still in shock. RCA in Marion covered the funeral expenses for all three of them. Many of Shannon's family members had worked at RCA throughout the years, and the owners felt it was the least they could do for the family during that tragic time.

As the funeral arrangements were made, family and friends began arriving from all parts of the United States. Everyone was full of anger and sorrow. One evening, several of Shannon's brothers and cousins gathered at Charlotte's salon to get haircuts and just enjoy each other's company. They reminisced about all the cherished moments and memories they had of Shannon and her children. They also discussed different ways to kill Xavier Hudson. One of the older brothers, Edwin, who owned his own barbershop in Indiana, was cutting his youngest brother's hair. Jay was waiting for his turn to get his hair cut; all of a sudden he yelled, "Edwin, look out!" as a rat ran from behind some boxes and scurried toward the chair where Edwin stood. Edwin lifted his foot and stomped the rat dead.

"That's how I feel right now. I want to kill those bastards who did this! I want to stomp them dead." He sat down.

Everyone was feeling the raw emotions that Edwin had just displayed. As the day of the funerals came, their anger and fear grew. Eddie and his cousins and brothers-in-law decided they needed to bring protection with them to the funeral services. Although they now knew that three people had been captured and charged with the murders, they still weren't convinced that no one else had been involved. They all went to the funerals with guns under their suit coats. Eddie had a .38 Special and Edwin had a Colt .45.

The services were beautiful, with many flowers for each of the deceased. Great numbers of people came to the church; many brought stuffed animals and toys, which were laid on the children's caskets. All three caskets were closed, due to the extensive burns on the bodies. People cried and shouted in pain and anger throughout the services.

The men had no cause to use their guns at the services or burials. Shannon, Teresa, and Lamont Wilson were laid to rest that day, but their family suffered with the pain of their deaths for all the years to come.

——— ◆ ———

Xavier Hudson, Jamie Lincoln, and Dean Olmstead were all found guilty on three counts each of first degree murder. Jamie's trial was the first of the three, and she had agreed to testify against both Xavier and Dean at their trials. Xavier and Dean continued to intimidate and threaten to kill many people who were going be witnesses against them.

The Honorable Justice Booker sentenced Xavier and Dean. During his pre-sentencing speech, he said to the courts and the defendants, "In addition to this being a particularly heinous crime, the most heinous I have seen in my lifetime, it is also an assault on the administrations of justice." The judge was appalled at Xavier's and Dean's attempts to manipulate witnesses and threaten them if they testified.

Xavier Hudson was sentenced to three consecutive life sentences of ninety-nine years each. He is currently incarcerated in a Minnesota State correctional facility. Dean Olmstead was also sentenced to three consecutive life sentences, which he is currently serving in an undisclosed state correctional facility somewhere in the United States. Jamie Lincoln was also sentenced to three consecutive life sentences. She served her time at Shakopee Women's Correctional Facility, but was released after serving just seventeen years, in exchange for her testimony against Xavier and Dean, and for her good behavior while she served.

The family of Shannon, Teresa, and Lamont Wilson has grieved their deaths for over thirty-five years. Although they have managed to move through the years filled with anguish and pain, they will never forget the loving memories of their cherished loved ones whose lives ended much too soon—all at the hands of a manipulative, money-hungry murderer.

Christmastime, one year after the murders

After a day of sightseeing and shopping, Charlotte and her sisters were sitting with their chairs in a circle, sharing their fondest and most cherished memories with each other. When it was Gina's turn, she said, "Something is missing here."

"What are you talking about?" asked Candace, the youngest of the sisters.

"We have everything we brought here," Davina said.

"No, I mean Shannon is not here with us. She's supposed to be here." Gina began crying. Before they knew it, all of them were weeping for their sister. After a while, the oldest sister, Denise, dried her eyes and stood up in the circle.

"Hey, while we all know the terrible death our sister suffered, and we all miss her like God only knows, we must always remember: as long as we have undying love for Shannon and the joy of her memories in our hearts and minds, she is always with us."

Suddenly a glass fell off a nearby table. The women screamed— and then started laughing hysterically.

"Yes, she is with us," Charlotte said, smiling as she remembered all the times Shannon would sneak up behind her and scare the mess out of her.

www.ingramcontent.com/pod-product-compliance
Lightning Source LLC
Chambersburg PA
CBHW030753200726
48288CB00004B/1149